Smoke Macaw and Lady Rainbow

Smoke Macaw and Lady Rainbow

Antony Mitchell

Copyright © 2023 Antony Mitchell

The moral right of the author has been asserted.

Apart from any fair dealing for the purposes of research or private study, or criticism or review, as permitted under the Copyright, Designs and Patents Act 1988, this publication may only be reproduced, stored or transmitted, in any form or by any means, with the prior permission in writing of the publishers, or in the case of reprographic reproduction in accordance with the terms of licences issued by the Copyright Licensing Agency. Enquiries concerning reproduction outside those terms should be sent to the publishers.

Matador
Unit E2 Airfield Business Park,
Harrison Road, Market Harborough,
Leicestershire. LE16 7UL
Tel: 0116 279 2299
Email: books@troubador.co.uk
Web: www.troubador.co.uk/matador
Twitter: @matadorbooks

ISBN 978 1 80313 604 2

British Library Cataloguing in Publication Data.
A catalogue record for this book is available from the British Library.

Printed and bound by CPI Group (UK) Ltd, Croydon, CR0 4YY
Typeset in 11pt Minion Pro by Troubador Publishing Ltd, Leicester, UK

Matador is an imprint of Troubador Publishing Ltd

To my mother, who did her best under trying circumstances; to George, a fellow lover of antiquity; and to the Maya, ancient and modern.

Chapter 1

Gold and Water

It was as if a giant hand had once dug through the surface world, the resulting open cavern revealing water the colour of lapis. Across this limestone-encircled lake – or cenote – glided a canoe, its two paddlers listening intently to the beat of the hide-covered drum that set the rhythm. Though they possessed human limbs, they and the canoe's other two occupants had, variously, the heads of an iguana, a deer, a turtle and a scarlet macaw – the last a large parrot of red-and-blue plumage. Some rulers named themselves after this bird, and it was the Cosmic Turtle that carried the Mayan universe on its back. Here at Water in Stone, the creatures in the boat were re-enacting the crossing by the gods of the underground sea of the Mayan creation stories.

The deer- and turtle-heads ceased paddling and let the canoe drift the last, brief distance to the cenote's centre. Downing their water-tools, the paddlers rose from mid-vessel and hoisted a sturdy pole with short cross-poles. The speed of the iguana-headed drummer's dancing hands increased. The macaw-head began to carefully climb the pole, one rung at a time, the step-bearers bracing their legs against the canoe's sides to minimise any rocking. After mounting the small platform at the top of the pole, the macaw-head remained in a squatting position for a moment to centre his gravity, before slowly erecting himself to his full height. The sun, too, had risen; high enough for its gaze to penetrate the dim light of the cenote. The macaw-head's body shone as the solar rays illuminated his form, the gold dust on his skin reflecting the light. The spectators on the underground shore drew in an audible breath as the creature atop the platform removed its hook-beaked head to reveal a human face painted in the startling colours of a macaw, a large white ring around each of the man's eyes mimicking those of the bird. Laying his macaw mask on the platform, he looked up to the sun and lifted his arms, placing his hands together.

"Oh, K'in," he called from his distant perch above the middle of the cenote, "today we honour you, whose daily journey across the sky guarantees the continuity of all life. Therefore, from this holy cenote, we ask that, at the end of this 360-day cycle, you spare us the terror of those five additional, mysterious days; that period of temporal instability and potential cataclysm."

The words echoed around the cenote. Silence returned.

The man stepped to the platform's edge. Slowly, he leaned forward; then he let himself fall, executing a dive of perfect physical symmetry. The impact of skin against water drew away much of the gold dust. It remained suspended briefly near the surface, like a shoal of fish deciding its next move, then disappeared into deeper water. The honourer of the sun swam back to the canoe, which, in its turn, rejoined the people waiting along the shore.

Once disembarked, the man-macaw's companions also revealed their human heads. The solemn protocol of ceremony was set aside too, as – shed of transforming beak, scales, antlers and carapace – the previously supernatural participants in the ritual were greeted and praised by their families and friends. The macaw-face and his brother – the canoe's drum-beater – gripped each other's shoulders in affection.

The spectators who had been high up in the cenote – watching from rope ladders, or from boulders along the cenote walls – compared their lofty experiences with those whose shore position had presented a somewhat 'flatter' view of the ceremony.

All present felt relieved of fear. The ritual that had just been performed would ensure that K'in, in acknowledgement of this rare gift of gold – almost never seen in the Mayan region – would initiate a new cycle of his movements and predictable positions above the Earth, or Middle Realm. The gods of the Underworld, also acknowledged in the ritual, would aid the passage of this people's ruler, when deceased, across Water in Stone and his descent into Xibalba.

Unnoticed, his grey cloak the same colour as the background of rocks, the shaman-priest Jungle Tortoise began to ascend the cenote wall. Once he was atop a large boulder halfway up the wall, all were suddenly aware again of his presence.

He spoke. "Subjects of Place of the Quetzal[1] Serpent, you have just witnessed K'in's glorious brightness reflected

---

[1] A red-chested bird with long green tail feathers.

in the gold-dusted water of this cenote. Know that – in a distant, volcanic lake to the south, in the high mountains of Kol Um Bah – there are other watchers of the sun. In an annual ceremony, their ruler casts precious objects of gold into the lake. Then, like our King, he dives from a raft of balsa wood into the cold waters of the Lake of the Golden Man. The people of Kol Um Bah follow their ritual by shaping gold into a miniature of the raft, bearing ruler and oarsmen, thus immortalising this act dedicated to solar continuity."

In awe of the creativity-in-piety of the people of Kol Um Bah, and inspired by Jungle Tortoise's words to a sense of solidarity with them, Quetzal Serpent's people felt strengthened further in their confidence in the future.

Chapter 2

Eyes of Green Stone

Atop the palace steps of Quetzal Serpent, King Smoke Macaw was lying in an adapted fishing net strung between two posts. It was a design of Jungle Tortoise's, and an exclusive gift from him to his King, though Jungle Tortoise had heard that islanders called Carib also used such hanging nets to relax or sleep in.

Smoke Macaw felt slightly dizzy after the rigours of the previous few days. To acquire the most aesthetic diving posture, he had hung upside down for long periods from a flexible frame, his back arched lightly and his fingertips touching the ground – "so that your form, thus trained, is beautiful when you enter the sacred underground waters," Jungle Tortoise had advised him. The physical and psychological purification in a steam bath, the resulting perspiration later adhering the gold dust to him, had dehydrated and weakened him. The painting of his face and eyes – the first stage in assuming the identity of the bird –

followed by the dedication ceremony accompanying the donning of the mask, had taken one complete night. His body now thanked him for this time of inactivity. His deeply relaxed eyes were shaded from the sun by a structure roofed with palm leaves, open-sided to accommodate any breezes.

Smoke Macaw sat up in his hammock to view his city and the natural features around him, recalling the extent of his lands. Before the palace lay the high plateau, sided by steep, forested mountains. Along the plateau stretched orderly groups of thatched huts adjacent to fields of food-plants. From where the plateau ended, a broad hill descended to the vast, flat area of scrub forest that stretched to the north. This hill had excellent defensive qualities. Anyone approaching Smoke Macaw's city from the scrub forest – as his own expedition had done when returning from the lowland cenote – could be seen from the ridge above, where two permanently manned stone towers were located. Amid thorny bushes and crumbled, strewn rocks was the one track up the hill from the low plain, permitting travel only in single file; the steep climb sucked much of an approacher's energy even before they completed the ascent. Only one intruding party had managed to fully penetrate the stockaded, funnel-shaped killing alleys at the plateau's end and, in rebuttal of the defenders' best preventive efforts, destroy life here – plant, animal and human – before itself losing much blood and being driven back down the hill. On a day without haze, the coast could be seen, two days' walk away to the east.

The palace-temple complex was painted a deep red, the blood-like colour bestowing upon Quetzal Serpent power both political and religious, though here more spiritual. Moreover, these buildings radiated their redness in bright sunlight, as today, the flaming colour aweing both the local populace and visitors to the city. Behind Smoke Macaw's palace was the pyramid-temple, and then a last field of maize. Beyond this, the claustrophobic foliage of a strenuously winding path led down another hill to the end of his lands, terminating in lowland rainforest. This forest was cut through by the river White Water, its source the distant, towering mountains abutting still-active volcanoes.

Smoke Macaw's brother, Twin Iguanas, entered the temporary awning. Twin Iguanas was one of only two people Smoke Macaw considered to be unwavering of character in a world that had often been at war with itself: brother opposing brother (here, the irony was not lost on Smoke Macaw), cities raiding their neighbours, and the Maya's overuse of the natural world's gifts to them.

Twin Iguanas knelt, arose again, and began his report. "My King and brother, I have news, some of it... of great surprise," he announced.

"I am listening, Twin Iguanas," said Smoke Macaw. He leaned forward, drew in his knees and cupped his chin in the palms of his hands, assuming the posture to be seen in carvings of deities.

"I, the War Chief and the warriors have returned from our punitive mission – you remember that we had no choice but to reaffirm our fierceness to that one city that is restless in its desire for antagonism."

Smoke Macaw remembered well. During the preparation for his stay at Water in Stone, images of his enemy had, like a strong wind buffeting a butterfly, more than once blown off course his purer thoughts of ceremony. Now, no longer focused on spiritual matters, he again had the luxury of time to wonder about the fate of his men who had waged mock war at the riverside city of Black Stone.

"As a warning to Black Stone," continued Twin Iguanas, "we toppled some of their standing, engraved stelae that honour their warrior Queen, and we set fire to the outer walls of the city. The people of the fields who, roused from their sleep, ran out of their huts in alarm, we kept silent upon threat of instant death, though, as you always command, my King, had they disobeyed us, we would have retreated rather than crush defenceless beetles beneath our feet. Indeed, we were betrayed not by them, but by our own arsonist flames that revealed our bodies in flight, spears seeking us out as targets."

Hearing this, Smoke Macaw felt even more deeply the incongruity between the unassailability of his own present location and the dangers faced by his men that night. He rose from the comfort of his hammock. "From our seeds of intimidation, then, have we reaped a partially blighted harvest?" he asked, wondering if precious lives, as he often called them, had been lost.

"We suffered only light wounds," answered Twin Iguanas.

"Smoke Macaw is proud of the leadership shown this night by Twin Iguanas and our War Chief," declared the King. "Our warriors, too, have served Quetzal Serpent well. But have you not something more to tell me – 'of great surprise'?"

"Yes, my brother. As instructed, we took no war captives. Nonetheless, our party became one more in number, for, upon our return, we found a person of high rank wandering through the scrub forest halfway between here and Black Stone. She can be brought to you now, if you wish."

"She?" echoed Smoke Macaw. "Could this woman be a warrior of Black Stone, separated from her patrol?" He was intrigued, for he knew of only one woman who actively engaged in armed conflict.

"I have watched her closely," answered Twin Iguanas, "and certainly she has a warrior's spirit. She showed no fear when we chanced upon her, nor once lowered her eyes during her escorted journey here."

"I am greatly curious to meet this chance 'prisoner,'" said Smoke Macaw.

Twin Iguanas clapped his hands in command. The woman was led into Smoke Macaw's reception chamber by two warriors. Now that she was in the presence of their King, the warriors forced the woman's level gaze downwards by pushing on the nape of her neck. The three of them neared Smoke Macaw, though with clumsy and uncourtly steps as the captive struggled to look up. Once directly before the throne, she was permitted to again raise her head.

Smoke Macaw momentarily stopped breathing. His hitherto composed face showed awe... and softness. The woman's features changed, too. Her look of defiance slowly evaporated, like the early morning mist above the warming forest. Her green eyes – an anomaly in the Mayan world – were like jade, thought Smoke Macaw; and, together with a bar of lapis lazuli through each earlobe and a redness in her well-developed cheeks, gave her a head of many colours, inspiring her people to call her 'Green-Eyed Lady Rainbow'. Smoke Macaw found himself trying to ignore a feeling that he had not experienced before: the intense wish to gaze upon a beautiful woman disrobed.

Finally subduing the inner combatant, his tongue once more became the servant to his thoughts. "I am Smoke Macaw, King of Place of the Quetzal Serpent. I hope that my men were not too rough with you." He looked for raw wrists (a sign of overly tight bonds), and for bruises or cuts that would tell him if she had been handled like an uncooperative prisoner. He was relieved to see no such evidence.

"Your concern for the well-being of someone completely unknown to you makes you truly worthy of the title of King," she replied. "But you are not unknown to me," she added. "There is an encaged impatience in my breast, ready to leap out of my mouth and relate how Lady Rainbow, daughter of King Parrotfish, came to stand before you."

Upon Smoke Macaw's signal, cushions were placed on the floor, and the Princess sat before him.

"Resolved to leave the hearth, father and city that had nourished and loved me to womanhood," began Lady Rainbow, almost breathlessly, "I hoped to find shelter at Quetzal Serpent. I knew that this temple city, its King famed for his epoch-changing approach to rulership, lay somewhere inland, atop a plateau so inclined that the mountains behind seem to retreat yet further the more one nears the plateau. Seeing this wonder for myself was a confirmation to me of the rightness of my decision to seek out this blessed part of the Middle Realm. I now feel sure that the gods had decreed that we meet, Smoke Macaw, for men of yours found Green-Eyed Lady Rainbow, self-exiled Princess of New Dawn, and brought her here."

"Quetzal Serpent and its King welcome you, Lady Rainbow," declared Smoke Macaw. "Our hospitality I offer to you in bowls and goblets served with joy."

"Your joy is my blessing, Smoke Macaw," she replied. Then the flood of words issuing from her became a rippling stream, their pent-up energy dissipated by Smoke Macaw's calming tone. "Despite my present happiness," she said, slowly now, "my life energy is low, and my tongue too heavy to cheerfully converse further. I would be quiet, alone. Yet I shall not feel the chill of loneliness, being warmly swathed in the contentment that comes with" – she paused, not wishing to seem presumptuous – "finding a new home."

"I will discipline my impatience, Lady Rainbow, as I wait to be honoured by your presence once again," Smoke Macaw answered. Then he added, reassuringly, "My abode is your abode, for as long as you wish."

The Princess and the King exchanged quiet smiles as she rose and left the room.

Chapter 3

The Heart of the Jaguar

Queen Death Bat and her small group of men stopped at the foot of the forest-covered slope. Would they be able to enter and retreat from the city above, she wondered, before the burning ball of day was once again seized by the nocturnal jaws of the Celestial Jaguar?

Something more immediate also made her question the wisdom of this enterprise: rising out of the leaf litter before her were two erect snake heads in stone, each taller than a man. Their long, pointed fangs were painted greyish-white at the base and red at the tips – the respective colours of poison and blood – and thus left no doubt that this was not only a territorial demarcation, but also a warning to outsiders. The only way up the mountain was behind these threatening forms. Watching the motionless snake heads, Queen Death Bat felt her muscles twitch in suspicion as she motioned her men to continue. The narrow trail curved regularly from one side to the other and often dropped suddenly, giving some of the men the deeply disturbing impression that they were being slowly churned and digested along the intestines of a giant snake.

After a great ascent, the trail widened. In a clearing in an area of level forest, the trail terminated at two large stone rattles – the tail section of the undulating snake. *Perhaps the snake is in the middle of a post-feasting sleep*, thought Queen Death Bat, *for the tails, like the heads we saw earlier, do not stir at our approach.*

A short distance behind the rattles, a massive stone slab announced the name of the ruler here, the stela engraved with the double glyphs for 'macaw' and 'rising smoke'. Leaving the forest, the party entered an area where maize, the life-giver of the Maya, could be seen growing on tall stalks. The Maya believed themselves to have been created from this "most beautiful flower". The gods had formed the first people out of muddy earth, but they were dissolved by the next rains. The second race of people were made from wood, but did not understand the significance of their own creation, and ran up into the trees, their descendants becoming the first monkeys. The perfect, true Maya people had finally been born when the gods used sacred maize.

Queen Death Bat was surprised to see no commoners' huts here. *They must be somewhere on the other side of the temple, but why so far from this food-growing area?* she asked herself. Perhaps to protect the fieldworkers from intruders like herself, she guessed with a smirk. Whatever the reason, she determined to make use of the emptiness here to act unhindered and quickly.

She and her men wore green-and-yellow body paint, which had allowed them to blend in well with the sun-dappled vegetation of the forest. They were similarly camouflaged here, against the backdrop of the maize fields. The drying lumps of crusty, coagulated paint pulled at their skin, causing an itching that was hard to ignore. This discomfort was nonetheless preferable to taking the risk that bare skin would pose. To benefit from reduced visibility, they gladly made this minor sacrifice.

They first walked outside the field of maize, but kept close to it. As the edges started to thin out, the party merged with the denser central stalks of the crop, as a flock of birds of one mind effortlessly and fluidly changes direction in mid-air. The sound of their occasional disturbance of the stalks blended in with the gentle rustling of the breeze. They entered the area beyond the maize field, exposed except for three towering *yaxche* or silk kapok trees, that seemed like sentinels, ready to interrogate any trespassers. As the *yaxche* played a fundamental role in Mayan cosmology, the trees' presence here was clearly intended to offer special protection to Quetzal Serpent. The party looked around nervously.

In supplication, Queen Death Bat addressed the trees, praising their greatness. "Oh, *yaxche'ob*, you are the bearers of the heavens. Your mortal forest crown, in this season covered in lilac-coloured blossom, holds in place the constellation of the Milky Way. Uniting the three worlds, your trunk transfixes our Middle Realm and your roots point the way down to Xibalba."

Directly beyond these trees stood a pyramid-shaped construction with a broad base and curved ends: Quetzal Serpent's temple. Now without the cover of forest or maize, the men paused behind the broad trunks of the *yaxche* trees – not touching them, out of fearful respect. They looked around them for a final time and then, having sensed the readiness in her body and needing no words of command, followed their Queen as she loped forward and started to ascend the temple steps. Their gradient and vertical spacing forced the climbers to spread their arms and legs to redistribute their weight; the group of human bodies now resembled a troop of spider monkeys. These warriors, like all Maya, saw it as an act of devotion to master such difficult temple steps: the approach to the sky.

Reaching the second level of the temple, the party faced a corbelled arch: one end of a tunnel. Passing through the tunnel, they wondered if they were running a gauntlet; the diluted daylight revealing vaguely to their eyes two muralled walls alive with scenes of astrological creatures including a scorpion, a turkey and a fish. Facing the opposite arch was another flight of steps, less steep than the previous ones. Queen Death Bat and her now-huddled group quickly climbed this.

The top level, a terrace and temple building, was higher than the forest canopy, causing a momentary sense of vertigo in several of the party. Peering through the double-entranced room of the *Kul Balam* – the Sacred Jaguar – Queen Death Bat could see three figures on the front terrace, their details obscured by the smoke from the torchwood tree incense burning around them.

"Move now," she said to herself, and entered.

There, on a stone platform in the centre of the room, was what she had come to find: a life-sized wooden carving of a standing jaguar, painted bright red, its body studded with dozens of pieces of lapis lazuli and jade, their outlines recreating instantly recognisable major constellations of stars. In the middle of the Sacred Jaguar's back was a depression lined with mother-of-pearl. Resting here was a carving of a human heart, made of layer upon layer of pink-orange spondylus shell from the coastal waters.

Queen Death Bat stared at the object. This was the Heart of the Jaguar Lord, the ultimate symbol of the divinity of this city's ruler and his dynasty's descent from the most powerful animal in the forest. It was now only an arm's reach away from her. She hesitated, suddenly held back by an awareness of the sacrilege she was about to commit; her face began to glow with perspiration at the thought of retribution from the supernatural beings she was sure dwelt inside this temple. *Is my fear a presentiment of a divine punishment to come?*

Slowly, half-expecting it to burn her desecrating hand, she lifted the Heart from its resting place. Her men, too, were becoming uneasy: she could see them outside, moving their heads erratically, stooping and squinting as they tried to follow her movements through the thickening, fragrant haze. The party were a long way in both space and time from the grass of the temple's rear approach, and discovery was a threatening spectre that could take solid form at any moment. Though King Smoke Macaw was known as a ruler who did not kill readily, the penalty for a transgression of this magnitude might nonetheless be death.

Still hidden from the three ceremonial participants by the Sacred Jaguar and the incense smoke, Queen Death Bat started to back out of the room. Then she stopped: through a gap in the human-made clouds she could see a womanly face, perfectly sculpted. "I am surely in the presence of a goddess come to visit this temple and witness its ritual," she whispered to herself. She could not move her eyes away; they were held by the mesmerising power of beauty. She waited to see if the face's expression changed, if its eyes registered unexpected movement in the chamber of the Sacred Jaguar, but the Queen could see no sign of being startled on the face that had caused her to temporarily forget her purpose here and almost drop the Heart.

Though she wanted to linger and prolong this sensual moment, Queen Death Bat knew that K'in, the sun, would grant to the Middle Realm only a little more of his light. The Queen and her party began a speedy descent of the temple's rear steps, scraping their bodies against the steep blocks of stone, yet in their urgency registering no pain.

Chapter 4

Smoke and the Rainbow

King Smoke Macaw and Lady Rainbow were walking side by side along a forest trail skirting Quetzal Serpent. His hand rested upon her shoulder with the lightness of a leaf, as if to not burden her further after her recent hardship of the storm and the humiliation of the trek across the plain as a captive. They talked of their pasts and presents.

She was the only daughter of King Parrotfish, ruler of coastal New Dawn and Eastern Rock, the latter a nearby island outpost. Her mother, like herself a woman pained at the thought of lifelong compromise, had left New Dawn, not sharing – as she had judged it – King Parrotfish's complacent, parochial attitude, and New Dawn's consequent isolation from the vivacity of the rest of the Mayan world. She had remarried, entering a household of rank in a city beyond the cenote of Smoke Macaw's diving ceremony. Lady Rainbow had not seen or heard from her since.

New Dawn had only a small population and Eastern Rock was little more than a settlement of fishermen. Both polities were poor in riches, and their remote location, accessible only by lake or sea, meant that they were of little appeal to any potentially predatory city states.

Lady Rainbow spoke. "One of the city's warriors, Bone Drum, asked my father if I might become his wife. Our territory is not large and my father always feared that a lack of appropriate suitors might one day cause our people to whisper of me as 'the Princess of the Barrens.'" She looked away a moment, reflecting on the less-than-noble appellation. Then her eyes met his again. "Such a title," she explained more fully, "recalls that least fertile, most inhospitable part of the scrub plain; the dwelling place of clouds of gnats, biting flies and mosquitoes around stagnant pools."

"Such an address to any woman," commented Smoke Macaw, "and especially one such as you, Lady Rainbow, reduces the importance of the spoken word to that of dust."

Her eyes shining, she bowed. "Reluctantly, my father agreed to Bone Drum's request. I, however, felt only repulsion for my suitor: though he is the most respected warrior in New Dawn, his features are not pleasant to behold, and he is violent even towards his friends and family. We know that the River of Blood foams and rushes into Xibalba, but through my body meanders the current of a royal lineage; powerful in its essence, yet measured in its flow. Thus, I lay claim to the right to choose the man for my life; a man who knows when to be calm, reaching for his spear only when himself mortally threatened."

"Your sanctioned bondage to Bone Drum," said Smoke Macaw, "would be unnatural and chaotic, for the storm and the rainbow always struggle for the greater spectacle. Yet the one must follow the other: the seven colours may only be seen after the fury of the air has spent itself."

Upon hearing these words, Lady Rainbow was reminded that, as much as she was drawn to his eyes and form, she also admired Smoke Macaw's succinct expressions of universal truths. *A rarity in a young man*, she thought, *even of high birth.*

She continued her narrative. "Unable to persuade my father to revoke his decision, I decided I would leave New Dawn. Before the meeting of night and morning, when I was sure that all were sleeping, I launched a fisherman's canoe from a section of the beach partly hidden by boulders and far from the watchtower. Though a child of these waters, by night the sea was as a stranger to me. Nonetheless, I had reason to smile: the brazier light from the watchtower that I had carefully avoided now served as my reference point. I used it to help me to avoid straying too far from the shore as I paddled along the coast. The watchtower light gradually became smaller with the distance. Then it was the glare of torches burning outside the occasional group of clifftop huts beyond New Dawn that provided me with a means of judging distance to the sand and the rocks. Soon I was moving through the water at speed, confident of my general direction and comfortable in my strokes. My sense of freedom gave me as much strength as the victuals I consumed regularly. For much of the rest of the night, I used the position in the sky of a familiar constellation to maintain my course with a minimum of deviation.

"It was a little before dawn when the sea and the air suddenly became angry, working against me. A strong current pushed me further away from the land and the wind lifted water into my canoe, slowly filling it. Then another player joined in this test of my determination and skill: seeing failure slowly overpowering my escape, hope seemed, out of pity, to take my side. It was the sky, K'in. A knife of light ripped through the clouds. Though my ears were shocked by the sound of thunder's impact, my eyes were soothed, for the briefly illuminated night allowed me to see the coastline. Thus newly orientated, I regained my course by paddling at a sharp angle through the current's side, alternating often the direction of my resistance, for I knew that in a direct confrontation with the power of the sea I would be the loser.

"As I neared the coastline, I could see that it had changed. Here were stunted, root-like trees growing in shallow water, their arched limbs seeming to bow to each other in harmony. When I saw an incongruous gap in the mesh of trees I steered the canoe towards it, and it revealed itself to be a narrow channel. I entered it, happy to be near the anchorage of the trees, which I could hold on to if need be. *Perhaps*, I thought, *I am entering a sanctum where the approaching storm is forbidden to follow, finally leaving me untouched.* I was right. Paddling became easier and, as I had desperately hoped, waves no longer splashed into my canoe; I could see that the barrier of trees was resisting much of the water's push.

"So concerned had I been with fleeing the threatening sea that only now did I become aware of the rain. My skin and hair were as wet as if I had swum through the channel. My arms felt as if, like my heavy paddle, they were made of wood; my victuals were almost used up; and, suddenly become a baby again, I could have lain down to sleep at that very moment. But to do so would have been to surrender at the very gates of victory, as well as a gesture of ingratitude to K'in. It was these thoughts that gave my arms new strength as they again wielded the paddle. The sky flashed more powerfully, rewarding my fresh resolve, and I could make out an inner shoreline. More of that night I cannot recall.

"When I awoke, it was day. Despite my damp clothes and the still-wet wood of the canoe, the storm might have never been, so warm was the sun and so still the air. I saw that the coastal lagoon had fed into a wide lake. Standing in the canoe, I could see, in the distance beyond the lake shore, a flat landscape with mountains in the background. I prayed in thankfulness for the benevolence of the gods and my ancestors: they wished me to complete my journey, I was sure now. In my excitement, I announced loudly, 'I am nearing Smoke Macaw's territory, and somewhere on the plain before me is a slope leading to the plateau of Quetzal Serpent.' I paddled onwards. From time to time I heard a violent disturbance of the water around me, and from the corner of one eye I registered a large, dark form then submerge, but I kept my eyes fixed on that part of the horizon where the lake, plain and mountains converged.

"The end of my journey was heralded by the sudden profusion of reeds, their thin yellow stems topped by white heads resembling fly whisks. My canoe bumped into the lake shore. Before harbouring it among the reeds and grass at the bank, I used my knife to carve a message into the canoe's wooden sitting-block. I read aloud this record of my landing, to reassure myself that I had not dreamed all of these events. Wary of the possible reappearance of the dark form half-seen earlier, I stooped and refilled my gourd with lake water, and, perhaps because I was so desperate to drink, I found its slightly salty taste surprisingly refreshing. Then forgetfulness visited me a second time. Thus is my mind empty of the events between my leaving the lake and being escorted here by your men."

"I feel privileged, Lady Rainbow, that you have shared the story of your epic journey with me," said Smoke Macaw. "The pull of the sea was strong but the push of your will was stronger. Few warriors could have shown more endurance than you showed that night. I bow in deepest respect to you, Princess of New Dawn."

"I thank the King of Quetzal Serpent for his kind words," replied Lady Rainbow. "But please, return the pleasure: speak now of yourself. What is your history?"

"The various city states," Smoke Macaw began, "had fought continually for generations: at first content with conducting raids to obtain live bodies for sacrifice to the gods, but then engaging in wars, severing the fragile strands of the spiderweb of Mayan interconnectedness. Internal aggressions added to the existing external ones, and the naked, deforested land could no longer feed the underfilled bellies of the overfilled cities. Long periods without rain and the ensuing thirst and hunger unrobed the priests and Kings of awe in the eyes of their people; those once divine seeming now merely mortal. This royal and religious impotence, and the Middle Realm's rebellions against humankind, were interpreted by all as the Great End Cycle of the Mayan calendar that foretold the destruction of our world – though, in fact, at a far later date. The Maya were sure that their lives would soon be taken from them during this astronomical period by the unstoppable laws of the cosmos. Finally, the Great End Cycle was perceived to complete its revolution, as the people's temples and fields were devoured by the Earth Monster rising from the earth, unchecked by the roots of a single tree."

He paused, the echoing silence impressing doubly upon Lady Rainbow the import of his words.

"First Dynast Jaguar Phallus was my father," continued Smoke Macaw. "After his city was destroyed during the presumed Great End Cycle, he and a large group of survivors travelled for many days, looking for a fertile, defensible location in which to live. One day, they saw rising from the low plain a sloping block of landscape, dually sided by mountains. The magnificent setting overwhelmed Jaguar Phallus; it beckoned to him. Already exhausted after the long traverse of the plain, small children were carried up this natural bridge connecting different worlds on their parents' backs; the weak, elderly or sick were aided by the warriors and the young. These people knew that there was nothing to return to: redescent would be as futile as a deceased ruler asking the demons of Xibalba for mercy. Ascent signified hope. Thus were they able to ignore their hunger, to shrug off their weariness.

"Their sun-blinded eyes were relieved as they beheld, on the other side of this bridge, a soothing green. A rich carpet of soft grass awaited aching feet, and the breeze bid the people welcome. Their exodus from chaos, the sense of effort shared during extreme circumstances rewarded with success, would be retold many times and with special fondness. Jaguar Phallus pointed to a tree before them, that peered down on the route they had just traversed. The tree was sparsely foliated at this time of year, revealing clearly its limbs. Everyone wondered at what they saw: two red-chested birds with delicate yellow beaks and green plumage. One had a double tail, also green, as long again as its body. The birds were making short, regular swoops, flapping their wings and then returning to their branch. After watching a few of these aerial displays, the people could discern the object of the birds' attention: a large snake, its head raised above its coiled body. Movement on the branch, but nearer the trunk, explained the snake's concentrated stillness: trying to hop and flap up the trunk was a small, vaguely furry cluster. It was a downy chick that had either dropped out of its nest or made a premature first attempt at flying. Again the parents harassed the intruder, their squawking and the male's quivering double tail distracting the snake and causing it to lunge only half-heartedly at the insubstantial and elusive streaks of green, the double tail alternately shimmering then fading confusingly as it turned in the sunlight. Unable to outmanoeuvre the chick's protectors, the predator finally gave up the hunt, sensing that it was spending excessive energy to acquire a minimal meal. Uncoiling, it gripped its branch with its tail, let down its long body and transferred itself to a lower branch, increasing the distance between it and its harassers. A bush adjacent to the foot of the tree allowed the snake to travel the short distance to the ground and slither away.

"Jaguar Phallus spoke. 'My subjects, after the fall of our city, our future seemed hopeless. Our ascent of the slope today was harder than any temple steps, with no promise of a new life for us at the top. Yet, on this branch above you, you have just witnessed cooperation and tenacity rescue a life from almost certain death. This I take as an inspiration to start here our new dynasty. Like the threatened chick aided from above, we will, with help from our wisest ancestors and gods, cheat death. I am breathless at the beauty of these birds, these flying jewels; too, I admire the suppleness and fluid movement of the snake. In honour of both, I will name our new city… Place of the Quetzal Serpent.'

"His words became reality. Working in mud and heat, he helped his people construct their huts, and lifted with the stonemasons blocks of limestone for the palace and temple."

"And how did your father otherwise lead in his new city?" asked Lady Rainbow.

"He made a simple comparison, telling his people that life cannot be lived like a ball game consisting of alternating attacks and reprisals," replied Smoke Macaw. "These were Jaguar Phallus's words: 'For present yet indecisive victories inevitably come later losses, and the player's price for losing at the ball game may be his head. So, too, may a King and his nobles put at risk the future of their city state, in their arrogance eventually playing it away. We Maya must not bring about before its time another Great End Cycle; only the Calendar of the Sky may prophesy where and when all things cease to be, and when a new cycle may start.'"

"I see dark clouds in your eyes that I take to be pain," said Lady Rainbow, Smoke Macaw's sadness evident in her own voice. "Where lies the body of Jaguar Phallus, spring of the semen that seeded Smoke Macaw's own greatness?"

Smoke Macaw's answer came in a quiet monotone; he was repeating aloud a memory he had relived so many times that scalding tears had eventually been replaced by the cool resignation of fact. "His life ended, with those of a group of his men, near or at Black Stone. They had travelled there to discuss a peaceful alliance between the two cities. They never came back. Messengers sent to enquire as to my father's whereabouts returned with the official statement that Black Stone had received no recent visitors from Quetzal Serpent."

"So you believe your father was sent before his time to face the challenges and horrors of Xibalba?" queried Lady Rainbow.

"Queen Death Bat's father, Ball Court Lord," answered Smoke Macaw, "was in our lands a skilled and undefeated opponent at *pok ta pok*, the ball game. Traders who lost the game had to give up their valuable wares for barter of smoked forest meat, shell jewellery, or chocolate pods in exchange for their lives; even Totonac – among the best players – sometimes lost to Black Stone, with slavery their fate if they had no wares with which to buy back their freedom. Black Stone thus became rich, materially and in reputation. I believe my father and his men were forced to play the ball game and lost. Ball Court Lord surely did not respect someone like my father: a mild ruler who neither conducted raids nor performed human sacrifice."

The King and the Princess talked further, now of more peaceful things. Then they fell happily silent. As Smoke Macaw gently pulled Lady Rainbow nearer to his side, an iridescent blue butterfly, each wing the size of a human palm, flew towards them, changing direction only a wing's span from their faces. To the people of Quetzal Serpent, the appearance of the blue morpho butterfly was an omen of good fortune.

Smoke Macaw turned Lady Rainbow towards him. As they were not at court, he wore no ornamentation on his head, and his hair, black and shiny as obsidian, was pulled up in the customary high topknot.

One of the gods surely struck his head at birth with a mace of that volcanic rock, thought Lady Rainbow as she wondered at the glassy lustre of his hair. She admired, too, his saliently sloping forehead; a sign of beauty in Mayan men and women, achieved by placing a wooden board on the baby's head and leaving it there for a time to reshape the still-soft skull. His form reminded her of the brocket deer: slender and agile.

Her eyes are suffused with starlight, thought Smoke Macaw. *Her nose curves gently; her lips are full. As the water at the beach cannot resist the pull of U, the moon goddess, so am I drawn to this woman.*

They kissed. His tongue drank deeply of her, like the hummingbird that intimately probes a flower for nectar. Breathing in his scent, she became doubly alive, her blood flowing with the strength of the hurricane at sea. Finally they slipped apart, albeit only slowly. Both wondered if many cycles of time had not passed; they could not be sure, for the disappearance and reappearance of a star could be measured in time, but not the duration of a kiss. One thing they did know: she would not – could not – leave Quetzal Serpent.

"The liana vines of our separate lives have met on the trunk of the Tree of Life," said Smoke Macaw.

"Yes," agreed Lady Rainbow. "The wrong union" – and here she thought of Bone Drum – "is like a tree that has become a permanent, though unwilling, host to the strangler fig, to be finally smothered by the vertical offshoots of the parasitic visitor. We, however, being of mutual understanding, will enjoy a wonderful symbiosis, with only our loneliness dying, and that a happy death."

Chapter 5

A Vision in Blood

At the top of the temple, Lady Rainbow was kneeling, Jungle Tortoise and Smoke Macaw standing at her sides.

Jungle Tortoise addressed her. "Princess Green-Eyed Lady Rainbow, cherished visitor from another city, each night, before preparing to dream, you have watched the moon and stars from atop the temple, safe under the aegis of the Founder Ancestor, Jaguar Phallus. Just as one's guest is beckoned to sit in privileged comfort before the hearth fire, so you have received welcome without reserve from Quetzal Serpent's people, and you have bathed in the adoration of our King, Smoke Macaw. Thus have you become part of us and we part of you. Do you wish now to strengthen your ties with us; to know the creator of all that you see here?"

Lady Rainbow nodded gently.

"Then, Lady Rainbow, honour Jaguar Phallus, us and yourself with a holy summons. Use the strength of your will and your body to endure the fear and pain that will allow you to communicate directly with the Great Ancestor, Founder of Quetzal Serpent."

Lady Rainbow gazed in admiration at the harmonious symmetry of the temple, the palace and the plateau. She took in the tightly packed mass of expectant citizens assembled down on the grass square. Finally, her eyes lit up as they came to rest upon the face of Smoke Macaw. Though encouraged by his presence, she nonetheless felt weak and was in a state of nervous agitation: the days of preparatory fasting and regular draughts of fermented maguey cactus juice, imported from the drier lands of the north, had given her mild hallucinations.

Gaining mastery over her quavering voice, she replied to Jungle Tortoise, "Yes, my priest, this I will do. The life of King Smoke Macaw and his city have become my life. Let my blood now flow in honour of this." She had in fact witnessed, during a private ceremony a few days before, Jungle Tortoise shedding his own blood in her honour. Thus, no less could be expected of her now, here upon the city's temple.

Smoke Macaw raised a long torch and placed it before her eyes; a second, blinding sun. Lady Rainbow held up the long, pointed tail spine of a stingray. Her eyes opened wide as she pushed a third of the spine through her tongue, then withdrew it and let it fall to the floor, its sacred function fulfilled. Through the hole in her tongue she carefully pulled a thin cord of vine interspersed with small thorns; again, she uttered no sound, only shuddered at the initial pain. The blood thus set free fell into a ceramic bowl containing a large piece of tree-bark paper, on which were painted the glyphs of a jaguar head and a phallus. Jungle Tortoise waited briefly for the paper to be anointed by absorption of the Princess's blood, then took the torch from Smoke Macaw and set alight the paper.

Lady Rainbow swayed involuntarily as she stood up and raised her head to watch the self-sacrificial liquid smoke rise towards the sky. The smoke took a definite form. After some moments, she announced with difficulty, her injured tongue and delirium causing her to stutter, "I see it. The two-headed… Vision Serpent… is opening wide its jaws. From one set of jaws… is now emerging… the head of Jaguar Phallus."

That Jaguar Phallus had left his world to answer her summons from this one was a sign to all of the Ancestor Founder's approval of Lady Rainbow as the future co-protector of Quetzal Serpent.

Chapter 6

The Shadow of the Heart

Jungle Tortoise reacted to the scene of the desecration without anger or fear; such emotions could not ambush one who had spent his life emptying his mind of debilitating emotions through deep meditation, and strengthening his body by regularly practising demanding postures. He also ate little, and eschewed meat and alcohol. This regimen facilitated his preparation and performance of regular public ceremonies. A mild quickening of surprise in his veins was the only stimulant he felt in his otherwise calm state. He looked long at the Sacred Jaguar. The mother-of-pearl depression, usually hidden by the Heart, was shiningly bare.

"In the last days," he said to himself, "the ever-watchful birds in the trees have, it seems, chirped too loud of our self-distracting preparations, the wind blowing their concert of voices to our enemy's ears. I – we – have acted like an overly confident warrior who, in the calm between battle charges, too long averts his eyes, keeps lowered his shield, and while drinking from his gourd is fatally surprised by an enemy missile that comes out of seeming nothingness. So too has Quetzal Serpent dropped its guard, and a stealthy claw has used the opportunity unwittingly presented it to enter the temple and sever the Heart from the Jaguar's body."

The other Mayan cities and settlements held in awe and feared the unearthly powers attributed to the Heart of the Jaguar Lord, for without these powers, they reasoned, how could Quetzal Serpent have retained its integrity without blood sacrifice? It was believed that the shaman-priest Jungle Tortoise was omniscient; that he had – in a different incarnation – once walked at the side of the creator gods, and the high priests of other rulers looked to him for inspiration.

Only moments ago, upon completion of the bloodletting ceremony, Lady Rainbow had collapsed with exhaustion, Smoke Macaw catching her in his arms. Jungle Tortoise had bidden him to take her to her chambers for rest. Smoke Macaw had borne her only a short way down the temple steps when Jungle Tortoise called to them. Though she lay limply in Smoke Macaw's arms, her arms hanging at her sides, Lady Rainbow's eyes were open. She managed to raise her head in wonder at the ageing astronomer-priest who was descending the ungainly temple steps with the agility of a much younger man.

"The Heart of the Jaguar is now held in unclean hands," announced Jungle Tortoise.

Smoke Macaw and Lady Rainbow looked at each other, the shock in their eyes written as clearly as stone glyphs.

"We now see, Smoke Macaw," continued Jungle Tortoise, "that your father's deeds, your own unbroken rule, and my revered name among priests were not enough to protect the Heart here for all time. Without its source of life, it has only a twentieth of its power. Your subjects will say that their King can no longer defend them; that their shaman-priest can no longer correctly interpret the configurations of the stars."

"Yes, Jungle Tortoise," agreed Smoke Macaw. "And I feel sure of where the trail of theft leads: to the city of Black Stone. My whole being tells me that the Heart is there; I know of only one who could enter the temple unseen, on the silent wings of a hunting owl: Queen Death Bat. She now holds the Heart, unnaturally, and has drained our city's blood. If we do not reunite the Heart with the Jaguar's body, then the political heart of Quetzal Serpent, the dazzling red of its temple-palace complex, will be held as no more fearsome than the laughter of children. Other Mayan cities may unite to descend upon us and reduce Quetzal Serpent's proud standing-stone structures to rubble, just as leafcutter ants devour the greenness before them, leaving bare once-vital trees. Jungle Tortoise, only you can know when the time is right for us to take back the Heart."

Jungle Tortoise knew that before retrieving the Heart a ritual of appeasement to the Ancestor Founder would have to be performed. Only then could First Dynast Jaguar Phallus pardon the carelessness that had permitted the Heart to be taken; only then would his wisdom continue to guide Quetzal Serpent.

Chapter 7

The Priest and the Princess: A Shared Vision in Sleep

It was the day after the bloodletting ceremony. Smoke Macaw and Lady Rainbow had slept long; she in his hammock and he on a reed mat on the floor of the same sleeping chamber. In her dreams, Lady Rainbow had seen something: nebulous in form, yet powerful. This sacred entity had travelled the pathways of Quetzal Serpent and probed its temple.

As if he had been listening in on Lady Rainbow's mumbled recollections to Smoke Macaw and come to clarify them, Jungle Tortoise appeared at the entrance to the chamber. His words, though quietly spoken, fully roused both sleepers. "My King, last night I was visited in my sleep by the spirit of the Sacred Jaguar of our temple. Through closed eyes, I saw it moving restlessly around the wooden image of itself that should still be holding the Heart."

Lady Rainbow breathed in deeply – she and Jungle Tortoise had dreamed the same.

"Once awake," continued Jungle Tortoise, "my open eyes revealed to me the significance of this deity entering the night-world of my head: it was a message concerning what had befallen the Heart. I know now what must be done: Smoke Macaw and the jaguar must meet. Balam must be brought to our temple and dedicated to Quetzal Serpent. This act of devotion will heal the wound inflicted upon the Heart, Balam's presence reuniting the spiritual axis of Quetzal Serpent with its severed limbs: the Ancestor Founder, the King, the priest and the subjects."

Smoke Macaw took Lady Rainbow's hand. "My future wife, I must prepare for my journey into the Forest of the Jaguar, that place where Balam feels most at ease, far from the habitations of men, who sometimes run him down and steal his beauty."

Lady Rainbow knew that – despite, and yet because of, their godly status – jaguars were still hunted by other Mayan city states. Rulers wore the whole pelt of a jaguar, an energy-imbuing symbol of their own semi-divine status, to justify and perpetuate their political power. Over the years, jaguars had become much less numerous, and had retreated to an area of forest between White River and the volcano Burning Mountain.

It grazed and bruised Smoke Macaw inside to think that he too might soon be required to cut short, via sacrifice, the life of one of these magnificent beings; he could almost feel in his own body the jaguar's death tremors to come.

Smoke Macaw will soon leave the safety of his city and the sureness of my love, and expose himself to the terrible claws and jaws of Balam, thought Lady Rainbow. She lowered her head; she did not want the sight of water in her eyes, as if drawn up from a cenote deep within her, to weaken Smoke Macaw's resolve. As ruler of Quetzal Serpent, was he not also a father to his people? *Whether human, fish or bird, a parent must first think of its young, not its mate*, she accepted.

Smoke Macaw turned to Jungle Tortoise. "Must I spill the jaguar's life-fluid?" he asked, fearing the answer.

"Our Ancestor Founder wishes only a gesture of our dedication to him and to Quetzal Serpent. He is not insatiable," replied Jungle Tortoise in a reassuring tone.

Smoke Macaw breathed easily once more, becalmed.

Chapter 8

The Forest of the Jaguar

It was late afternoon. The tree-crowns now acted like thickening clouds, blocking the light trying to reach the Middle Realm.

In a glade, Smoke Macaw rested his spear against a sapling and took the travel basket off his back. He knew jaguars to be most active at night, so he would use this period before twilight to begin baiting, and prepare a fire for his comfort and safety. He had brought tinder with him: light, fluffy fibres from the pods of the *yaxche* tree. For kindling, he now collected twigs of various sizes from the branches of the trees – twigs from the damp ground would not burn. The bark he removed from the still-dry combustible wood inside with his hipknife. Finally, he cut slim logs with his longknife, also removing the bark. The sound of his hacking and chopping would – he hoped – alert Balam to his presence. Before lighting the fire, a firebreak was necessary. He fashioned a simple broom and cleared tree debris well away from the area. As well as giving him warmth in the cool of the night, a moderately sized fire would bid caution to any jaguar that might consider approaching the sleeping human. The fire was also symbolic: the centre of the Middle Realm, from which emanated the four world directions.

To aid his eyes in the approaching darkness, he ignited a slow-burning torch, fuelled by oil from the nut of the cohune palm. From the basket he took three darts with blunted ends; only the small flint tip of each was sharpened. He opened a ceramic pot containing curare, the cooked bark and root of a vine used as a powerful tranquiliser by the peoples of the Endless Forest to the south of Kol Um Bah. It had taken from one rainy season to the next for the ingredients to travel from there to the Mayan lands, so great was the distance. He dipped each dart-tip into the resinous black fluid and then dried the darts over the fire. His stomach began to tighten with hunger. He unrolled the large mat he had brought with him and sat cross-legged to eat the pemmican and dried fruits prepared for him by Lady Rainbow. He thought of her and was lovingly thankful for these comforts she had provided. Eating voraciously, he chuckled at the thought that she might be shocked to see him, a man of refined manners – a King – tearing at and devouring meat like a wild animal.

Time for light thoughts was limited here, he knew, so he began to plan his next actions as he waited for the world to change from one of many reassuring colours – the greens, blues and yellows of the daytime forest and sunlit sky – to one of only two colours – the darkly blinding night-time forest and the white points of stars visible through gaps in the canopy. When the once-familiar forms around him started to blur in clarity, he knew his prey's time of activity had arrived.

He picked up the spear, the pointed end facing the ground, attached the torch to the haft end, and left the fireside. Walking back along the entrance trail, he urinated several times against the trunks of trees, laying claim to territory just as jaguars demarcated their own – a provocation to Balam, demanding an active response. Smoke Macaw reached into his palm-frond shoulder bag and withdrew a calabash gourd, the fruit-shell from the tree of the same name. The wider end of the gourd had been cut open and deerskin stretched over it. The narrower end had also been cut, and from this opening an armadillo tail was suspended from a cord knotted through the deerskin. The tail was sealed and preserved in specially hardened beeswax. Smoke Macaw stopped often, thrusting the spear-point down into the forest floor to hold upright the torch. Holding high the drum end, he plucked at the armadillo tail, whereupon a deep, muffled grunting issued forth. From time to time, he modified the tone, stroking the tail to produce a more open utterance, closer to a cough. "Variations in sound will awaken the interest of both male and female jaguars," Jungle Tortoise had told him.

Smoke Macaw also manipulated the jaguar-summoner while walking along side trails, knowing that jaguars often rested in such places, in hidden beds of flattened grass. Then he retraced his route and lay down next to the fire. "I can easily refill my water gourd at nearby White Water, and jaguars do not usually travel far from their riverine or swampy homeland," he reminded himself sleepily. "I will continue to call out for Balam tomorrow."

The roaring of howler monkeys shook him out of his happy dream of Lady Rainbow.

"So high up in the trees and woken by the sun's first movements, you have surely been active a long time already," Smoke Macaw called up into the tree. "As for me, it may be that I have slept too long and allowed the jaguar to return to its resting place after a night of hunting."

The grey-green shades of the forest, however, reassured him that the morning was still very young and he would, therefore, have another chance of luring the jaguar – a good chance, in fact. The forest here was densely populated with jaguars; for two reasons, one pragmatic and one spatial. This area was relatively far-removed from human habitation, Black Stone in particular being potentially perilous. Too, expansion of jaguar territory beyond the dwarf-treed, prey-poor high mountains and riverless volcanic landscapes would have been difficult. Thus, here was a large number of jaguars to be found in a limited area.

From the glowing embers of the fire, Smoke Macaw relit the torch, which would now function, if necessary, as a second, more passive weapon, complementing the aggression of his spear. He had an additional strategy that would increase his chances of luring a nearby jaguar. He took out a piece of uncooked meat that had been kept moist by wrapping it in leaves. This he pierced with a twig spit and held part of it over the remains of the fire, using a large, sturdy leaf to waft and disperse the fragrance of the lightly grilling meat. Now he placed some embers from the fire in an aerated ceramic pot, and replaced the lid. This he would carry in one hand, and his torch-spear in the other. The meat he rewrapped in the leaves and then packed in his shoulder bag, along with the spit. His portable grill was ready. He walked again towards the river, making several stops to repeat the actions of briefly grilling the meat and wafting the smoke. *If a jaguar is anywhere nearby*, he thought, *it will detect the smoke and hopefully try to locate the source of this unusual-smelling meat. Its surprise will be immeasurable when it discovers a man, and not carrion burned by a fire in a glade.* He knelt and drank from the river, his spear at the ready, his eyes and ears alert, then returned to his base and relit the fire, now become only ashes and remnants of fuel-wood. He then traversed the three other world directions, sending to the jaguar more messages promising meat.

Having tried to use scent as a lure, he decided that he would again use the medium of sound. A hilly trail led him to a natural clearing above White Water. Growing close to the edge of the ravine was a broad tree with thick branches; its trunk leaned out over the escarpment. "This tree seems to have been born to serve the Kings of my lineage," said Smoke Macaw. "Held in its mighty arms, I will try to communicate with many jaguars simultaneously."

The tree's first branch was too high to reach with a jump. Unlooping a length of rope from his shoulder and cutting it, Smoke Macaw fashioned a harness around his hips and loins. He wrapped a section of rope around the trunk, tying off the ends through the harness. Moving his eyes several times from his body to the tree, he was satisfied that the distance between them was correct. The tree, the rope and he were now one. He began slowly to ascend the trunk, alternately lifting and pulling for hold on the left and right cords. He constantly checked his centre of gravity and kept his legs bent at the knees, at the same time bracing the length of vine against his back and leaning out slightly from the trunk. Lifting, pulling, bending, bracing and leaning – each movement had to be precise and in sequence with the others, as any inconsistency could result in a fall.

As boys, he and Twin Iguanas had scaled straighter, taller trees in this way, feeling like human spiders as they 'walked' up and away from the world of soil and grass and into the airy realm of the birds and other dwellers of the trees. During one ascent, Twin Iguanas' rope had snapped and he had fallen – only the relatively short distance and the chance positioning of the brothers' cloaks and baskets at the tree's base had cushioned him as he landed. From that time on, Jungle Tortoise had forbidden them to indulge in any further 'spider-walking'.

Smoke Macaw soon reached the branch. He disengaged himself from the harness and dropped it at his feet. Tensing and relaxing in turn the muscles in his limbs, torso and neck, he shook off the stiffness that had built up during his climb. Realising that he had left the jaguar-drum at the river when refilling his water gourd, he decided to instead try using his throat to send his message. He cupped his hands to his mouth and roared many times. The roars, like those of the spider monkeys he had seen earlier, carried across the narrow ravine; this vocalisation was quite different to that produced from the jaguar-summoner the night before. Nonetheless, he was optimistic that any deep, loud sound uttered from his throat could be used to make appear an otherwise invisible jaguar. To a bough he tied one end of the rope, making knots in the remainder of its length for a comfortable descent.

"Jungle Tortoise has said that Jaguar Phallus has evenly measured expectations of me regarding appeasement," recalled Smoke Macaw. "Surely, then, my return to the Middle World needn't be as strenuous, and therefore as virtuous, in the eyes of the Ancestor Founder as an ascent towards the Upper World?" He raised his eyes questioningly to the sky.

Using the knots as steps and handholds, he descended the tree. Once on the ground, he stopped to reflect on his efforts. "The urine markings and meat-smoke are meant to arouse the territoriality and hunger of the local jaguars. The vocal summoning has hopefully convinced them of the presence of both a sexually competitive male and a potentially receptive female. Will Balam come to determine who or what is newly present in the forest?" With a jerk, he loosened the hanging slip knot, causing the rope to fall from the bough to his feet.

Back at the now-dead fire, Smoke Macaw sought a low tree from where to carry out the final phase of his plan. Such a tree he found at the glade's edge, half-hidden behind some palms. He thrust the spear-cum-torch lightly into the trunk at an angle to hold it there, and waited. Over time, his eyes discerned ever more differences in colour, pattern and shape within the apparent confusion of greenery around him. His initial impatience had disappeared completely; he now experienced total acceptance of whatever might await him, be it success or failure.

He heard the jaguar long before he saw it: a growling similar to the one he had created with the jaguar-summoner. "Unable to ignore my messages," said Smoke Macaw, "the jaguar is now seeking contact. At last, an encounter with the Middle Realm manifestation of Balam, where human strategy competes against animal cunning."

A bush seemed to move by itself, and a cluster of low palms to shimmer. One small area of green parted. The camouflage of vegetation melted away, revealing slanting eyes of pale honey set in a large head of orange-yellow fur, the face and ears rounded yet angular. The jaguar god had made himself visible. He raised his head and sniffed the air. Reflecting the sunlight, the neck and breast gleamed white. *Balam is formally announcing himself*, thought Smoke Macaw as the mouth opened in a snarl, revealing an upper and a lower pair of curved canine teeth; a lethal counterpart to the human's knife.

Balam's earthly appetite had clearly been sharpened by the drifting grill-smoke, for the jaguar slowly approached the piece of half-cooked meat lying on the ground. Once again imitating its kind, Smoke Macaw coughed. The jaguar looked up, growled, then returned its attention to the meat, sniffing the end that was still bloody. Smoke Macaw coughed again, whereupon the jaguar transfixed him with its eyes. The width of the jaguar's back legs prevented Smoke Macaw from determining its sex but he guessed that, if it was a male, he had just registered an unmistakable challenge to his territory. If female, her unnerving stare might be an expression of anger at not encountering a potential mate as the source of the calls and the food.

Smoke Macaw, his head also lowered now so as not to openly challenge the jaguar with his eyes, moved slowly away from it and towards the tree. At the trunk he turned and, eyeing the jaguar, ascended quickly, removing the spear-torch on his way and holding it by its middle in his mouth to keep his hands free. In contrast to the tree at the ravine, this one could be ascended effortlessly, gratefully naked of encumbering ropes and harness. He had barely reached the first branch when the jaguar appeared at the base of the trunk. "My retreat, though discreet, and my flight from ground to tree seem to have excited the jaguar's hunting or territorial instincts to the full," said Smoke Macaw to himself.

He placed the treated darts ready for use in the crotch of the tree. He knew that jaguars were able climbers, and, though attacks on humans were almost unknown, he nonetheless decided to reduce any enthusiasm for ascent on the jaguar's part by waving the flaming torch over its head. The jaguar moved away from the tree. Smoke Macaw picked up a dart. Keeping the torch in his left hand, and with the dexterity and speed acquired through much practice, he used one hand to place a dart in the dart-thrower, making sure his face and body remained turned towards the animal. Though apparently young and healthy, this might be a sick jaguar, unable to hunt its normal prey, and so willing to consider a human – especially in a moment of distraction – as an easy kill. It could, if it wished, leap upon him before he drew in a complete breath. Smoke Macaw leaned forward. Simultaneously, he pulled back his arm and then snapped it forward, releasing the dart. Hit in the shoulder, the jaguar roared – more in surprise than in great pain, Smoke Macaw suspected. The jaguar clawed and sprang at the trunk of the tree, but did not climb up it.

"All beings fear flames," Smoke Macaw reassured himself, "and the torch is like a wall between me and the enraged, much stronger jaguar below."

He used this brief period of non-engagement to load another dart, then launched it at the jaguar. This one struck the animal's back, and it roared again. Smoke Macaw's initial pride in his aim was, however, counterbalanced by dismay, for in his haste he had knocked the spear-torch out of his hand. It fell to the ground, the impact separating the torch-head from the haft of the spear. The jaguar's eyes filled with what the local Maya called 'the Warrior Fury': an unthinking, uncontrollable desire to destroy. It sprang to the upper trunk and clawed its way onto the branch where Smoke Macaw stood. Without his spear, he had only his longknife to fend off his opponent; this he unsheathed from his back, between the jaguar's last movement and its next one.

Smoke Macaw bent his knees to give him extra balance on the narrow branch. *If I fall now*, he thought, *the jaguar will almost certainly pounce on me. Having overpowered me, its canines will hold my head and crack my skull while its paws twist my neck and snap the upper bones of my back – a double death.*

The jaguar lashed out, the curvature in the movement of its leg and paw almost sweeping away the longknife.

One or two more similar attacks, and my longknife may be deflected sufficiently for Balam to spring upon me here, thought Smoke Macaw. He now snarled at the jaguar and, thrusting repeatedly with the longknife, shouted, "I am King Smoke Macaw, also of divine descent, and not to be defied. I am here to turn my shaman-priest's visions in sleep into the tangible form of a captive jaguar. The Princess Green-Eyed Lady Rainbow waits to fulfil her destiny as co-ruler of Quetzal Serpent. For all this, I must transport you, Balam, to the pyramid steps there."

As if these words had been blows from a club, the jaguar began to retreat. The look of the killer faded from its eyes and it turned away, leaning its torso over the trunk as it started to descend the tree. One of its front legs was already hanging limply, no longer able to support the animal's weight. The jaguar clawed at the bark with its other paws, trying in vain to control its descent. Jungle Tortoise had been correct: the curare had indeed slackened the jaguar's muscles and its body was not responding fully to the commands of its head. The normally fear-inspiring creature lay sprawled on the ground, barely snarling and unable to rise. Smoke Macaw watched from the tree, waiting patiently for the sedative to take effect. The jaguar's eyes were closed, its head and limbs unmoving. Smoke Macaw descended the tree; he could now start to bind the jaguar's limbs. First, though, it was necessary to check that the animal was still breathing. An overdose of curare could cause suspension of the respiration, and Smoke Macaw had no wish to in any way harm his erstwhile adversary; only to present her – he saw now the anatomical traits of a female – as part of a ceremony of goodwill to the Ancestor Founder and the Mayan gods.

Curare was only effective when it entered the bloodstream from the outside, and not when ingested, so Jungle Tortoise had produced several samples, determining the strength of each by tasting its bitterness with his own tongue. He had expanded on these findings by inserting curare-coated darts into captive frogs and observing how long they hopped before paralysis overtook them. His final test had been to stun a tapir, which had later recovered. In gratitude for its role in his experiments, he had wanted to allow this fellow forest-wanderer to go free, but then decided he could not justify such an action – fresh meat was not plentiful, so the tapir had been heavily sedated and then butchered in the city.

Carefully, Smoke Macaw watched the jaguar's chest and throat for signs of movement, and was reassured of continued, if much-slowed, breathing. He combed his hands through the jaguar's fur, traces of drying blood leading him to the two dart punctures. He cleaned the wounds antiseptically with extra-strong *balche*, a fermented drink of tree bark and honey. From his travel basket he took two sticks and a wooden cylinder. Each end of the cylinder was sealed but a longitudinal slit ran down its middle, for sound emission and amplification. Smoke Macaw sat on his mat and began to drum. "Summoning my men from the other side of the river is going to be easier and quicker than luring the jaguar has been," he reflected. "Yet, I am more than content, for my labours here have been well rewarded."

One contingent of his men arrived. The jaguar was laid with care on a litter and carried out of the forest. To prevent Balam's mortal body overheating, a large palm leaf was fanned constantly along its length, and water poured over its head and neck sparingly and intermittently to prevent shock as coolness met heat. The other contingent of warriors was waiting at the riverbank, watching over the canoes. Upon reaching the opposite bank, the canoes were lifted out of the water; compact and light, they could be easily carried back up to Quetzal Serpent. The group remained close together, with Smoke Macaw leading the way and one warrior as the rear guard, spear at the ready in case of ambush – Black Stone lay further down the river, and Smoke Macaw and his men knew the opportunistic, bloody credo of that city state's inhabitants.

Chapter 9

Resurrection

On the grass square in front of Quetzal Serpent's temple, a chattering crowd had gathered to welcome their ruler and his bearers. A group of noblewomen were exchanging compliments on each other's headscarves. An old man used the atmosphere of general excitement as an opportunity to flirt with some of them; he was, at this moment, raising the gown of an unaccompanied young woman, trying to expose her legs. She was unsure how to react, as men of long life were allowed to display normally unacceptable behaviour. From his eyes, breath and fumbling, she knew also that he was drunk.

The sound of voices ceased the moment King Smoke Macaw appeared. *As when the palm of a downturned hand opens, the stone therein drops to the ground*, the King thought. The relative orderliness of small conversational groups was replaced by the bustle of a disorganised crowd, whereupon the royal guards were compelled to cross their spears as barriers to prevent the swell of bodies from engulfing the returnees.

"Armed with enthusiasm but not trained in the protocol of welcome, the common people might unwittingly injure their King," observed the War Chief.

The crowd was ushered back by the guards. As Smoke Macaw passed by, his subjects lowered their heads for a few moments, though they quickly rose again to stare at the jaguar. This was probably the only time in their lives that they would see Balam, known also as 'the Elusive One', incarnate; even Jungle Tortoise had rarely encountered a jaguar in his forest wanderings, so ethereal was this creature.

The jaguar party arrived at the temple steps. Smoke Macaw remained still and looked long at the jaguar lying at his feet. Then he looked directly at the crowd, and with his eyes drew his subjects' collective gaze to the palace. Thus were all reminded of the bond between the Jaguar dynasty and its people; that only Smoke Macaw could be the rightful ruler of Quetzal Serpent. The even-toned murmur in response assured him that the wilted flower of loyalty was again swelling with trust and confidence.

The spectators were directed to seat themselves on the ground, noble and commoner alike. They drank water sanctified by their shaman-priest while waiting for the act of spiritual re-bonding to begin. Priestly attendants aided Smoke Macaw in the changing of his attire. He donned a billowing yellow loincloth patterned with dark rosettes – mimicking the fur of a jaguar – but he wore no headdress or robe. His lack of regal adornment, and the staff he held, topped with long ears of maize, served as stark reminders of the interdependence of even the humblest of subjects – the maize-gatherers – and their bounty-bestowing ruler. *Reciprocity is the lasting foundation of a city state*, Smoke Macaw reaffirmed to himself.

Twin Iguanas took his place alongside his brother. Jungle Tortoise wore a white skirt, but he was unshod, his chest was bare, and his hair hung free. *So he declares his connectedness to the untamed creatures of the mountains, forests and rivers*, thought Smoke Macaw.

Jungle Tortoise knelt before the jaguar and would remain closest to her for the duration of the ceremony, for it was he who would be best able to judge how to handle her when she awoke. "All creatures exhibit their own group-specific behaviour, but can still act unpredictably as individuals," he had told Smoke Macaw.

The spectators were again assembled before the temple. Musicians blew on long wooden trumpets to announce the beginning of the ceremony. Lady Rainbow was standing forward of her companions, holding Smoke Macaw's spear. The exaggerated size of its tip showed the ruler's readiness for war against his enemies, yet the frond of many small feathers below the tip gave the weapon a contrasting softness, reflecting that same lord's commitment to mild rule over his people. She held up the spear, to remind everyone present that she would become Queen, or act as Regent of Quetzal Serpent, should Smoke Macaw ever leave the Middle Realm without their having a fully grown heir to the throne.

The four privileged bearers lifted the jaguar into the litter and ascended the steps to the temple summit. The litter was placed on a platform projecting from the top steps. Twin Iguanas and Lady Rainbow descended to lower steps, Jungle Tortoise and Smoke Macaw remaining on the platform with the jaguar.

Jungle Tortoise addressed the people of Quetzal Serpent. "Subjects of Smoke Macaw, I, Jungle Tortoise, sent your King to the Forest of the Jaguar to find and bring back Balam. This he has done. We are known to the other Maya as a city that does not perform blood sacrifices; we show our remembrance and respect in other, less destructive ways. Today we will honour the Ancestor Founder Jaguar Phallus. The Heroic Twins of legend were forced by the lords of Xibalba, the Realm of Fear, to sacrifice each other, yet they later brought themselves back to life. The jaguar, too, will rise once again, here on our temple. This will demonstrate Balam's ultimate indomitability and confirm the immortality of his namesake, Balam Yat: Jaguar Phallus."

The jaguar's eyelids fluttered slightly. Jungle Tortoise hoped that he had calculated the dose of the curare accurately, and that his time spent in wild places had made him an intuitive judge of the individual character of an animal. The shaman-priest held up the black obsidian sacrificial knife. It glinted both in the sunlight and as he passed it in front of the torch, rotating the blade. He also passed the knife through the torch flame to purify it. For Quetzal Serpent's subjects, time seemed to have slowed to an unbearable pace, so great was the sense of anticipation. In slow motion, Jungle Tortoise brought down the blade toward the jaguar's head.

The priest did not slit the jaguar's throat. Instead, he held down her head with his knife hand, and with his free hand released the slip knots binding her limbs. Then he removed the wicker muzzle, Smoke Macaw holding the torch and ceremonial spear as control and defence.

How will the jaguar react, once awakened, Smoke Macaw wondered, *finding herself away from her home, and with blade and flames near her head?*

The jaguar began to move her head from side to side. Breathing deeply, she savoured the flow of blood that reached her limbs, now freed from their numbing bondage. Her whole body slowly regained its coordination. After trying to stand but falling again several times – "The night hunter as unsteady as a newborn fawn," murmured Lady Rainbow – her front and back legs finally became once again the servants of her will and the jaguar lifted herself up. The spectators below raised their arms in silent reverence to the reborn Balam. Smoke Macaw was their lord's personal title, but his father's legacy to him was that of the jaguar god. Witnessing Balam's rebirth here on the temple steps, the people of Quetzal Serpent were once again sure of Jaguar Phallus's patronage.

Seeking orientation, the jaguar looked around. She roared, the sound reverberating around the temple and palace area of acoustically designed, partially hollow steps and building blocks. Then she bounded down the steps of this curious, man-made mountain, devoid of plants or streams. Upon touching level earth again, she snarled as she was confronted by an array of human claws – handheld spears – that left as a route of flight only the maize field behind the temple pyramid. The jaguar unhesitatingly took this route, sensing that the trail would lead to the river and then her forest home. When she reached the snake-rattle portals at the top of the hill trail, she found a depression in the ground, its base layered with mortared pebbles for impermeability. The water buoyed fresh green leaves, and fern fronds lay scattered around the depression; these were considerations of authenticity, intended to mimic both the river surface and the riverbank. A mere bowl of bare ceramic containing well water might have been less appealing to the jaguar: the water not the freshest, and the container, from its unnatural appearance, obviously a product of the oft-suspect human hand. The benevolent preparers of this offering had wanted to be sure that the animal would drink before her long descent to the river proper on her way back home. Thus, the 'pool' here was filled with water from the river itself, newly carried up by the forest party. Close by was the body of a freshly killed domestic dog, with the jaguar's own scent upon it. Balam would need new strength for her swim across the river to the Forest of the Jaguar.

Chapter 10

A Weaving: The Heart, Bat and Stars

Nine Stars, the priest of Black Stone, was holding in his hands the Heart of the Jaguar. As he examined its beauty and felt its aura, he understood the respect it generated among all Maya. One half of his face twisted into an aberrant smile. "Now that the Heart is Black Stone's," he murmured, "some Maya of the region will become aggressively bold in their dealings with Quetzal Serpent, whose King's animal totem has been removed." Suddenly, he covered the Heart with both hands, hoping that this unearthly, sentient object had not registered his blasphemous statement.

Queen Death Bat entered the temple. She and Nine Stars raised their respective sceptres of office in ceremonial greeting. The priest placed the Heart in his ruler's hands.

The Queen looked deep into the Heart. "The walls of shell are dissolving under my gaze," she said. "I can see my future clearly. First, I will bring together the more ambitious and warlike of the Mayan leaders and rulers. In well-organised military campaigns – of my design – they will help me overrun Quetzal Serpent. Under the subsequent rule of Queen Death Bat, trade and movement of all peoples in the area will be controlled by Black Stone and Quetzal Serpent, using our two city states' combined geographic advantages of fast-flowing river and all-seeing high plateau."

She did not share all her strategies and acts to come with Nine Stars. Annulling previous alliances and creating new ones as often as the wind changes direction, she would also quickly subdue any challenges to her newly expanded authority.

"The settlements will be rebuilt and the small cities extended," she continued, "all becoming thereafter vassal city states of Black Stone. Massive stelae at their entrances will commemorate Queen Death Bat's victories and praise her monumental building programmes. New rituals will confirm me as the earthly embodiment of the star Lahun Chan (Venus)."

Venus was the most feared heavenly body, with its first appearance as the morning or evening star auguring drought or hunger, or being interpreted as a coming period of war. To pacify those of Venus's destructive qualities not exploitable to Queen Death Bat's advantage, the ruler of Black Stone would, to her own immense satisfaction, reintroduce human sacrifice; a practice fallen into disuse since the rise in influence of Quetzal Serpent.

"Naive rulers like Smoke Macaw have weakened the battle spirit of the Maya and ignored the gods' need for blood," she said.

Nine Stars nodded vigorously, sharing her conviction.

"Finally, my name will be remembered throughout all time as that of the first female ruler to create a true Mayan empire."

Queen Death Bat had registered the manner in which Nine Stars, with calculated deliberation, had transferred the Sacred Heart of the Jaguar from his hands to hers; too, he stood closer to her than usual, to confirm the inseparable relationship that existed between them – or so he believed.

"The high priest's knowledge of the heavenly movements and his unfailing devotion to the gods ensure the continued adoration of a ruler by the people," he reminded her.

In his words, flattery and self-promotion overlap, thought the Queen, *as do the sun and moon during an eclipse. I wonder if his ambitions are also of such a cosmic scale.* Her seeming agreement with his statement could be heard in her voice as she replied, in a familiar tone that was rare for her, "Nine Stars, it is time for you and I to initiate the decline of Quetzal Serpent. Have a messenger party sent there to announce that a ball game is to take place at Black Stone on the first day of the next month. Notify also the other cities and settlements of the forthcoming game."

"It will be done," replied Nine Stars. "Traders and visitors invited to the ball game will witness Smoke Macaw's humiliating defeat at the hands of Black Stone's players, and will tell their own rulers and peoples of our superior power. This will reduce the possibility of non-Mayan regions interfering in our – your – future activities, my Queen."

Queen Death Bat smiled and with a light gesture of the hand bade him to leave and carry out her... request, for how could she simply command such a 'cherished' priest, one whom she permitted – for now – to consider himself almost her peer?

Chapter 11

The Ball Game

The ball court lay in an area cleared of the surrounding scrub and not far from the cenote of Water in Stone where King Smoke Macaw had recently performed the gold-shedding ritual. In addition to the rulers, the settlement chiefs and their nobles-cum-representatives, here today was a rarely seen, compact assembly of the other strata of Mayan society: scribes, warriors, and people of the maize. Ready to watch the ball game, some stood, others sat under the shade of cotton awnings hung between low trees.

Smoke Macaw had rejected Queen Death Bat's selection of Black Stone as the location for the game, remembering that his father had never been seen again after visiting that city state. *Just as*, he suspected, *after the Great Decline, some of the new settlements were built strategically in or near forest plentiful in rattlesnakes, likewise might Black Stone be infested with traps awaiting myself and my team.* Thus, he had declared instead as the venue the more neutral location of Water in Stone.

The ball court consisted of two parallel, slanting platforms dropping off shallowly to level ground. Each was surmounted by a wall, along the top of which were three evenly spaced stone rings, through which a rubber ball had to be passed. Players wore a thick girdle, also of rubber, with which to rebound the ball from their hips, controlling its direction using discs attached to the girdle. The ball had to be kept aloft, the players running and passing it both in the level playing area and along the slanting platforms. To score one point, a player could hit one of the designated painted markings on the opposite wall; shooting the ball through one of the other team's rings, on the other hand, was considered the mark of an exceptionally skilled player and earned the scorer's team two points. The ball was bounced off most parts of the body – heavily padded – including the shoulders and thighs, but use of the hands and feet was not allowed. In some games, the ball's movements symbolised the orbit of a selected planet, and the game's outcome was used as an oracle to make important decisions. When victors in war played against the vanquished, the latter invariably had untended wounds and had been kept hungry and thirsty, and so had little strength to compete well. The captive team's poor performance could thus be predicted with certainty and, as the losers of the game, they were usually decapitated. Today, the prize and the loss would be different yet just as great, if Queen Death Bat's plan became reality.

The Bat team's wall presented as their target paintings their namesake creature of the Underworld, its head in profile and its wings extended. On each wing was an eyeball torn from a deceased ruler who, making his way through Xibalba, had failed the challenge of finding a way out of the

House of the Death Bat. The paintings on the Macaws' wall were of the skeletal Lord of Death, holding by its topknot a decapitated head with its tongue hanging out. Both sets of paintings reminded players that death could be waiting for the losing team, or at least its captain. After several game meetings, following which the paint would disintegrate from the impact of repeated ball-blows, men from Black Stone would come to repaint the bats in black and the eyeballs in white, and men from Quetzal Serpent to repaint the skeletons in white and the drooping heads in brown. To avoid spontaneous conflict between them, the maintenance teams had agreed to visit the ball court in different seasons of the year, vague in their precision; for example, one team would arrange to come during the dry season, and the other sometime after the harvest.

The two teams of four players faced each other in the middle of the court.

Queen Death Bat spoke first. "Smoke Macaw, if your team wins today, I will tell you the location of the Heart of the Jaguar. If your team loses" – now her voice became a dark melody – "I demand in exchange for your lives the woman I saw through the veil of incense smoke; she who made flow her own blood."

Smoke Macaw knew that the warrior Queen had no King who could adorn her future with children; however, instead of suggesting a marital union between herself and him, she was claiming Lady Rainbow as potential trophy. *Queen Death Bat feels herself drawn, woman to woman, to Lady Rainbow*, he understood from the look of desire on the Queen's face. Forever losing the Heart, Queen Death Bat's bizarre intentions towards his beloved, and the ignominy of his city's defeat at the ball game – all these possible outcomes shocked Smoke Macaw. He felt his spirit double spring involuntarily from his body. *What an achievement it would be for Queen Death Bat*, he reflected, *to keep the deifying Heart of the Jaguar; what a prize to acquire too Lady Rainbow, promised as a wife to the King of Quetzal Serpent. If I am true to myself, both as King and as a man, I cannot say what would scar me more: the loss of the Heart and my city state, or knowing Lady Rainbow to be encoiled in Queen Death Bat's unyielding arms – a boa's embrace.* To enable Lady Rainbow to return unscathed to New Dawn, he thought fleetingly of sacrificing both himself and Quetzal Serpent's independence by offering to become Queen Death Bat's husband. *Yet, to thus free Lady Rainbow would be to betray our love. Too, such an act of self-degradation would annihilate the dynasty of the Ancestor Founder, branding into my royal skin the glyph for high treason. The megalithic stela of disgrace would fall upon Quetzal Serpent, crushing its once-proud name.* Regaining strength from the knowledge that his intuition had served him well – he had correctly guessed Queen Death Bat to be the thief of the Heart of the Jaguar – he willed his spirit double to return to him, centring once again his self-assuredness. *I am fortunate that Quetzal Serpent is a city state of considerable resources*, he thought. *Queen Death Bat's words, overpowering in their resonance, might cast a lesser ruler into a wild river of self-doubt, to be finally engulfed by a whirlpool of despair.* Too, the thought of his ever becoming the sire of Queen Death Bat's surely venomous offspring – and here he recalled in analogy the time he had seen baby scorpions scuttling over their mother's body – led him to make a vow to himself. *I will meet head-on and turn aside any and all blows to our happiness, just as the rock pool below the waterfall deflects and disperses the pounding power of the torrent falling upon it.*

A calm determination overcame him. He was certain now that he would be sending Queen Death Bat's team back to Black Stone, their heads still attached to their necks but lowered nonetheless, as losers of the ball game. He turned his back to the Queen and brought his mouth close to Twin Iguanas' ear. "My feeling is that Queen Death Bat expects me to play little better than a mortal today, despite my descent from the gods. She knows that our players too are skilled at the game, so I ask myself why she is so sure of victory."

Looking over his brother's shoulder to watch the Queen, Twin Iguanas whispered in return, "My King and brother, Queen Death Bat will do anything to both claim Lady Rainbow and keep the Heart of the Jaguar. Since we are not her sacrificial victims, ritually bled and weakened before being dragged onto the ball court, I believe she has arranged for us to lose. It may be that she—"

The sharpness of Queen Death Bat's voice cut through their discreet exchange. "Here are your girdles and your pads. Prepare yourselves to compete against the most respected players known in the Mayan lands."

Curious, Smoke Macaw picked up and kneaded the leather and rubber protective clothing, and discovered it to be too thin and light for practical use as a shield against the dense, hurtling ball. He threw the unworthy armour to the ground. "As King of a temple city and as a non-vassal," he replied, "I refuse your request and reject these vestments. This old, worn leather is poor protection against a blow from a ball. The padding is clearly from a rubber tree of inferior quality; the tree old or diseased. My team will use its own pieces of bodily defence."

Queen Death Bat's team looked at each other – they had not expected this. No previous free opponent had dared question the Queen's prearranged selection of game clothing, and any suggestion of trickery on her part had been subdued by her imperious insistence.

Seeing their fall in confidence, Smoke Macaw pre-empted a face-saving command from Queen Death Bat, announcing, "We begin now, without niceties or protracted speeches; my people await with impatience our return. The rules we all know. May our children relate and their descendants read of a game well played."

Each team of four was distributed in a zigzag along and close to its own sloping platform. The pattern was the same as that of the sharp, abstract curves of the undulating rattlesnake carved at the top of the ball court's walls. Both the game and the rattlesnake had a dual nature: winning a game granted life to the winners and often death to the losers. The appearance of rattlesnakes in the dry season foretold that the rains would come to impregnate the maize seeds in the ground. Yet the same scaly messengers of bounty to come, when disturbed in the field by the planter-harvesters, could puncture the body with occasionally lethal poison. The judge, sworn to neutrality, wore a white robe and held two staffs of colourful feathers; his headdress was a fantastic, massively crested bird holding two fishlike forms in its long beak. The fish recalled the Heroic Twins of mythology. After losing the ball game against the lords of the semi-watery Underworld Xibalba, the Twins had been sacrificed and their remains thrown into the River of Blood. Nonetheless, they managed to fool the lords, using magic to transform themselves into supernatural catfish and resurfaced unnoticed. The mythical bird Muan had then carried them in its beak back to the Middle Realm, where they reverted to their human forms. Thus had the Heroic Twins ultimately defeated the lords of the Underworld.

The judge entered the court and stood in its centre, on a stone disc flush with the court floor and engraved with human figures – again, the Heroic Twins. In his hand was a black rubber ball the size of a large squash. Smoke Macaw thought he recognised the red glyphs etched into it, but it was not close enough for a clear view. Inexplicably suspicious, he would later examine the glyphs more closely, regardless of the game's outcome. The judge threw the ball high into the air between the opposing teams, then retreated. A Bat and a Macaw player leapt simultaneously, colliding as they failed in their attempt to intercept it. Another Macaw used his hip-girdle to direct it up into the area of the opponents' platform, where Smoke Macaw hit it with his knee onto one of the bat-eye markings. The judge raised the staff of blue feathers, from the plumage of the hyacinth macaw, declaring a point scored.

The ball was handed to the judge to throw and a new round began. In possession of the ball, two Macaws manoeuvred around the Bats and prepared it for relaying to Smoke Macaw and Twin Iguanas. The royal brothers completed the sequence, Smoke Macaw using his chest to bounce the ball against the target wall, to then pass through a ring. Again, blue feathers rose above the players' heads, eliciting both cheers and admonitions from the spectators. The Bats' strategy now was to use compact, continuous passing to penetrate the Macaws' side of the court. In this way, two Bats managed to push through the Macaws, whereupon one Bat hit the ball hard with his shoulder, aiming it at the ring. At very close range, Smoke Macaw leapt at an angle across the ball's path and, with his torso, stopped its further passage. Despite his leather tunic, the impact made him wince.

The game continued. Many times the Bats neared their opponents' markings and rings, only to have their shots blocked. Too, their lack of accuracy when aiming long or high caused them to fail to acquire points. When, in desperation, Queen Death Bat kicked the ball to cover more distance, the judge stepped among the players and raised his staff of scarlet macaw feathers, signalling a penalty point against the offending team. The Queen's angry features, her lips drawn back, reminded Smoke Macaw indeed of the snarling face of Zotz, the Death Bat.

During the next round, a Bat deliberately stumbled and fell to the ground. Using the visual confusion of compact, fast-moving bodies as cover, he furtively scooped up a handful of dust and threw it into a Macaw's face in an obvious attempt to blind him. The judge looked up and down at the dust-thrower with contempt. Had he been merely a spectator of this game, he might have laughed in ridicule at such amateurish tactics. His role here, however, permitted him no such freedom. He signalled a foul – another non-point for the Bats. One more non-point or instance of improper play by them, and the Macaws would win by default, should they not score directly. Animal calls from the spectators, only half-formed to show their disrespect, added to the Bats' frustration. They needed one paint-marking point and one ring point to match the Macaws, three points to win; however, their multiple and speedy attacks, all unsuccessful, had left

The Ball Game

them exhausted. Only Queen Death Bat seemed unaffected. Her natural inclination towards physical exertion left her feeling more refreshed the more she played; had the other Bats possessed her stamina, the Macaws might eventually have found themselves outplayed.

In the last round only the three central players – Queen Death Bat, Smoke Macaw and Twin Iguanas – remained. The other five had become little more than decorative pieces in the game, hovering at the court's edge. Though supple as a green shoot, and with reflexes as quick as a harassed fly, playing alone, Queen Death Bat was no match for her two equally skilled opponents, who kept the ball in motion and out of her reach, each time delivering a killing stroke and another point scored. More than once she managed to keep the ball, bouncing it from one part of her body to another, lithely avoiding her opponents, and finally shooting. But the ball's trajectories were never completed. The Queen's hope of victory, or even a draw, lay dead at the players' feet, Smoke Macaw and Twin Iguanas the executioners.

The judge raised both staffs to end the game. When he announced a clear win for the Macaws, Twin Iguanas did not hesitate to remind Queen Death Bat and her team of the significance of their defeat. "Just as the Heroic Twins outwitted the domineering lords of Xibalba, so have we today outplayed our initially arrogant opponents."

Most spectators roared in approval of a hard-fought game, smothering the few hisses of disappointment. The Macaw supporters expressed their good mood by imitating the loud, raucous squawk of their namesake bird. The teams faced each other, the judge standing again on the central disc between them. A scribe from each team would record the scores and the two rulers' closing statements. Queen Death Bat and Smoke Macaw stepped forward. He spoke first.

"Queen Death Bat, the gods and the Maya have just seen our teams play a ball game that will long be remembered. The Bats have been worthy opponents; exceptionally fast in their movements." As a sign of goodwill, he did not mention the Bats' less flattering actions during the game. Smoke Macaw stepped aside, acknowledging his competitors with a sweep of his open hand. "Now, as the victors' King," he continued, "I demand you fulfil your pledge and tell me the location of the Heart of the Jaguar."

"Smoke Macaw," replied the Queen in that same pleasing but semi-threatening tone, "you and your players have also quickened our pulses today, especially mine; my time playing alone against you and your brother was a rare thing, to be savoured as my gods savour fresh human blood. Now, your prize: to learn the whereabouts of the Heart." She paused. "It is in the deep waters of Water in Stone."

The lack of surprise on Smoke Macaw's face disappointed the Queen. He had suspected that she might place another obstacle in his path to retrieving the Heart. She must have somehow communicated the Bats' imminent defeat and, as no doubt previously arranged, the Heart had been thrown into the cenote – it was not far from the ball court.

"No mortal, not even a King, can possibly stay underwater long enough to reach the deepest part of Water in Stone," stated Queen Death Bat.

"I will retrieve the Heart," countered Smoke Macaw.

"The ball will now be given to the victor," declared the judge, but Queen Death Bat's hands continued to play with it.

"Where is his body?" demanded Smoke Macaw.

"It was discarded after he lost the ball game against my father, Ball Court Lord," answered Queen Death Bat. "We preserved Jaguar Phallus's head as best we could but the skin finally fell away; no doubt his spirit double's expression of weariness at waiting for the appearance of searching relatives."

It was true: Quetzal Serpent had not immediately made enquiries as to Jaguar Phallus's whereabouts, assuming that he and his group had remained for a while as guests of Black Stone.

"Jaguar Phallus came to you on a peaceful mission," said Smoke Macaw, "to exchange ideas and plans that would benefit both our cities. Your father's reception of him and his men was detrimental to both Black Stone and the new Mayan era. Remember, Queen Death Bat, all humans are connected. To urinate in the well of one's neighbour is also to sicken oneself."

Queen Death Bat smiled at Smoke Macaw's belief in long-term cooperation and restrained ambition. "His skull was mummified," she continued, "and kept for some years, waiting to be encased in tree resin should our respective rulers ever again play. As you may by now have guessed, his skull lies inside the ball we have just played with; a forgotten Mayan custom I believe we should revive." Here she casually tossed him the ball.

Finally, Smoke Macaw's composure strained visibly against the weight of his emotion. *Instead of this humiliating flight of his earthly skull through the lower air of the Middle Realm*, he thought, *should not my father's spirit double have long ago enjoyed its victorious journey across the sky after defeating the lords of Xibalba?* He caught the ball gracefully.

Cradling it, he studied the glyphs on its surface and pictured within not mere cranial bone, but his father's earnest, mild face, which had been unafraid of showing the earthquake tremors of emotion when his wife had died young. As a ruler Jaguar Phallus had felt especially close to his people, and had known the footpaths to the homes of the craftsmen and maize-gatherers, many of whom he had called by name. Still fresh for Smoke Macaw, too, were his memories of journeys of one or two days into the forest with his father, his brother and Jungle Tortoise to marvel at the sky-reaching trees and to find beauty also in the smaller things: the playful-looking coatimundi with its long nose and ringed tail; the basilisk lizard, its hind legs skimming its body across the water. All these things Smoke Macaw relived and, calmed, realised that he loathed not Ball Court Lord, but his deed. He did not ask if any of Jaguar Phallus's men had been spared sacrifice; of any enslavement, Queen Death Bat would surely have already spoken happily. Instead, he said, "Judge, I claim this ball for eternity as mine. Inside it is the one bodily reminder of my father's earthly stay. It belongs to Quetzal Serpent and our dynasty. Once again in its rightful place, his skull-spirit will have completed its journey of death by treachery and rejoiced homecoming."

The two team captains looked to the judge, who nodded in agreement. Each team was now at its own wall. While the Bats had to endure their Queen's haranguing, Smoke Macaw gave each of his players a mild, congratulatory fist-blow to the shoulder to indicate his satisfaction with their performance. Though disappointed at the Bats' overall performance, he was impressed by Queen Death Bat's agility, and turned to the facing wall, unable to resist comprehensively appraising the Queen's physical form and appearance. She was tall – the tallest woman he had ever seen – and leanly muscular. Her face, though lacking feminine softness, was handsome, and eyes that beheld it never forgot it. Charcoal lined her eyes, making them appear darker and larger. Her hair hung down her back, knotted around a human bone – judging from its size, perhaps a child's, thought Smoke Macaw sadly. Though her voice had something in it of the Underworld, and so of death, he decided that she was nonetheless a magnificent specimen of womanhood, as Jungle Tortoise, in his analytical manner, would no doubt have said. Smoke Macaw was forced to acknowledge that – though he was both her enemy and already betrothed – he nonetheless found her attractive.

Queen Death Bat turned; she knew she was being scrutinised. In response to Smoke Macaw's look of fascination, she relaxed her normally intense eyes and parted her lips, thrusting her face forward. Smoke Macaw was related to the gods, but he was also part mortal, and she could sense – almost smell – the game's dried, salty battle-sweat being replaced by the sweeter sweat of sexual desire. "Where will our orbits cross next time, King Smoke Macaw?" she asked seductively. "In my sleeping chambers, perhaps?"

Smoke Macaw, caught off-guard by her directness and unsure how to reply, turned quickly away. Seating himself in his litter, he instructed his party to leave for the cenote of Water in Stone.

Chapter 12

The Triton-Shell Call of Deceit

The messenger was Bone Drum, the warrior who had requested the hand in marriage of King Parrotfish's daughter. Lady Rainbow confirmed to her people-in-waiting that she knew him personally, and so he was led directly to her, without the questioning or ceremony that normally preceded an audience with royalty or a noble. He entered the palace room where she was seated on a cushion, reading Jungle Tortoise's *A History of the Maya*. She half bowed. Only when she did not straighten fully, but merely looked at him questioningly, did Bone Drum return the greeting, vaguely bowing his head.

She rose and, with an elegant gesture of her hand, bade him take her cushion, "warmed for your comfort, honoured guest.

"Welcome to Quetzal Serpent, Bone Drum," she said, ascending the receiving platform. "We last met two and a half full moons ago – for me a brief eternity. I hope you have since been granted by the gods a woman you desire."

His disappointing answer was the one she had expected. "My search continues. During each visit to a potential wife, I see not the woman in front of me, but the one your father granted me: you." He gave her a hard look.

Lady Rainbow's womanly warmth continued to radiate towards him, but he could not feel it, this man whose volatile nature had lost him the company of everyone he knew, save that of other warriors when on a mission. She tried to reassure him. "Show patience, Bone Drum. Love arises when it should. Like the sun, it cannot be accelerated into appearing."

His grim expression remained. "Lady Rainbow," he said, changing the topic, "your father's health has worsened suddenly. The healers cannot help him. He asks that you come to him – his next request may reach you too late for you to answer it with your presence."

It was true that she had fled from her father and her people – a fugitive from injustice, as she had perceived it – instead of departing as befitted a Princess. Now, in silence, she recalled her thoughts at that time. *My people are sea people but, should I drown in a sudden storm or be carried by unforeseen currents to an uninhabited part of the coast to die slowly, I will not see my beloved father again. As a person of high rank, I can die once in this life and perhaps a second time at the hands of the demons of Xibalba, but each day of marriage to a man not of my heart would be a new death; a black sun crossing the sky of my life.* The urgency of the present situation, however, greatly outweighed her emotional discomfort at the prospect of being escorted by her embittered former suitor.

"Bone Drum, we leave today for New Dawn," she assented.

Chapter 13

Men-Fish at the Cenote

Smoke Macaw and his party arrived at the cenote Water in Stone. As he had before the dive, he looked down from the edge of the cenote, but now with more scrutiny. Deep was the water, but from its clarity it did not seem as interminable as its association with the Underworld would suggest. *Where down there does the Middle Realm end and Xibalba begin?* he wondered.

He recalled a time when water had often caressed his skin. He and Twin Iguanas had sometimes played at the river-fed lagoon that lay beyond the bottom of the Serpent Trail backing Quetzal Serpent. They had been watched over by Jungle Tortoise and a party of warriors. Though not a swimmer himself – few Maya were, as bodies of water were sacred and thus could not be thought of as sources of pleasure – Jungle Tortoise had nonetheless encouraged the boys of elevated lineage to propel themselves across the water, "with arms and legs centred not unlike a frog's limbs, but moving continually". So had the young Smoke Macaw and Twin Iguanas learned to swim, with minimal instruction. Later, unable to control their curiosity and daring, they had started to jump and dive from trees fringing the lagoon, swimming confidently under the surface too. *The challenges of Smoke Macaw and Twin Iguanas were lighter then*, reflected Smoke Macaw. *Here we must swim deeper and stay down longer. Too, this cenote must seem foreboding to my men. To permit their terrestrial forms an initially familiar contact with the water here, they would surely welcome as gladly as long-unseen friends their canoes, which now lie sleeping at the lagoon.*

"I and Twin Iguanas," he announced, "will swim from the underground shore here out to the cenote's centre, for the Heart was surely thrown there, into the deepest part."

"My King, let us send for other supplies and equipment," suggested Jungle Tortoise, reading Smoke Macaw's thoughts. "We do not need the canoes. We have enough tools to work the raw materials to be found here in the scrub forest. We can build something that will give you more time underwater, without the need to resurface continually. A supply party can bring the few additional materials we will need."

Smoke Macaw looked long at his high priest, with fresh admiration. "Jungle Tortoise," he said, "you reveal to us wonders that equal the events of the creation myths transmitted by the Gods to the first Mayan shamans and copied down by them in bark-paper books."

All who knew him, or had heard of his activities, said that Jungle Tortoise was, by virtue of his inventiveness, an oracle of the distant future.

"Nor was I shy," replied Jungle Tortoise. "As you and

Twin Iguanas showed your love for the lagoon, I too became intimate with the water, in my own way."

With warmth rising within him at the past so recalled, Smoke Macaw nodded affectionately to the man who was not merely his city's priest, but, for him, also family. He addressed his men. "Men of Quetzal Serpent, some of you will work with Jungle Tortoise down here on the border of Xibalba; the others will accompany me to the Middle Realm above the cenote. There we will try to summon a support party."

Smoke Macaw led his group away from the cenote, and Jungle Tortoise began to instruct his. The subdued colours of the cenote walls and boulders were replaced by a violent blue sky, causing eyes to narrow. There was no haze – ideal conditions, in fact, for the men who would act as 'sky messengers'. A large fire was set. Placed upon it were mounds of grass and green sticks collected from under the trees. Dense white smoke arose. Next, cloaks and blankets, dampened to prevent combustion, were laid over the fire and soon after pulled away, releasing controlled puffs of smoke. Halfway back to Quetzal Serpent, a lookout in a temporary camp-tower erected on the plain would read the message, which would then be duplicated and finally received by the watchmen at Quetzal Serpent's ridge. Several types of smoke-message were commonly used. One puff signalled a need for food and drink only, two puffs in sequence a need for materials for construction, and multiple puffs a need for weapons and warriors. Any such silent message was later repeated to maximise the probability of its being seen; intense haze or low cloud sometimes camouflaged messages, rendering them invisible.

When Smoke Macaw and his party descended once more into the cenote, they found Jungle Tortoise's men already measuring, cutting and binding the materials they had gathered. Both parties' water gourds were collected and the largest ones set aside. The human-fashioned replaceable cap that covered the narrower, drinking end of each gourd was removed. A hole was bored into the other end and the snugly fitting end of a long pole inserted. The open end would then be lowered vertically into the water, trapping air inside the gourd.

"It is an amusing paradox," Twin Iguanas shared with his brother, "to see drinking vessels used to keep water out and air in."

Smoke Macaw had to agree.

Horizontal frames, later to become rafts, were constructed of branches and vine-cord. Large stones were bound to the centre and corners of the frames as balancing weights, and on each raft was erected a latticework tower, from the top of which Smoke Macaw, Twin Iguanas and ten others would dive. The rafts and gourds were tested in the shallower water near the shore; some gourds let in water and had to be discarded, but others retained the air within them. The natural form of these latter gourds, and their cutting and shaping, would serve as models for any later appropriated from the support party from Quetzal Serpent.

The support party arrived the next morning. They brought with them the requested food and cutting blades, as well as paddles and much-needed additional vine-cord – one raft had started to break up in the water when tested, having been insufficiently lashed together with what little cord was left.

With the last adjustments made, Jungle Tortoise checked the quality of the construction and was well satisfied with the men's work.

"Brother," murmured Twin Iguanas, "notice how different Jungle Tortoise is at this moment."

"Yes," replied Smoke Macaw, equally discreetly. "Usually, a remote expression is stamped upon his face, fired in the kiln of his deepest thoughts. However, his behaviour changes almost with the speed of a shooting star whenever we leave Quetzal Serpent, with its constant demands for his priestly counsel. There, his tasks are appointed him. Here, as at the lagoon in our younger years, he can feed the starving yearnings of his raw creativity. Earlier today, he granted us one of his rare smiles. Now, as then, I am happy to see the pleasure he is taking in seeing the drawings in his mind take physical form."

Once finished, the rafts were pushed out onto the water and paddled either closely along the shore, or to one of the cenote's sheer walls.

"I too do not believe," said Jungle Tortoise to his King, "that Queen Death Bat's men would knowingly leave the Heart in shallow water for us to simply retrieve. Nonetheless, we may save time and conserve energy by first exploring the upper reaches of the cenote. Many eyes have a better chance of connecting with the Heart." He could see that some of the newly appointed divers, despite their – albeit brief – training in swimming and diving, were still nervous about their proximity to the edge of the Underworld. They were not only about to leave the relative certainty of their solid world, but to enter at speed an unpredictable one that simultaneously resisted and yielded to the efforts of the human body.

Beginning the search for the Heart in shallower water, Jungle Tortoise decided, would give these novice swimmers a greater sense of security.

He boarded Smoke Macaw's raft, upon which a brazier of incense was already burning. As the raft crossed the water towards a wall, the shaman-priest recited a formula to appease the denizens of the Underworld in anticipation of the pending trespass from above. Smoke Macaw and Twin Iguanas ascended separate towers. They dived one after the other, followed by the rest of the divers. Aiding the bound stones that balanced the raft were the paddlers, who served as living ballast, countering both the rocking motion caused by those divers who left their platforms with an energetic spring, and the aquatic aftershock of the dives. As soon as the rafts were stable again, each paddler lowered a long pole – its separate, bound sections glued together with hardened resin – holding a gourd containing the 'small wind of life': air. Most of the divers quickly became used to the freshness of the water and the sensation of complete immersion. Too, they found that they were indeed able to comfortably refill their lungs from a designated gourd.

This world below the surface also challenged the strength and courage of the underwater searchers for the Heart. Each man could feel the pressure on his ears of the surrounding water, and more than once, a failed attempt at withdrawing air from a gourd compelled a diver to kick upwards and break the water's skin, this time from below; or there was simply no more air in the gourd and it had to be raised high on the raft and re-lowered into the water, full once more of the sustaining substance. As nothing made by humankind's hands was found near the shore, the rafts were repositioned in a circle at the cenote's centre. A second round of searching began, now at a greater depth. Radiating out from their lord, the divers scanned below them, hoping that the Heart would reveal itself to them, its intense colour contrasting with that of the water, now filtered by the clouds to a blue-green.

After watching yet more unrewarded activity on the part of the divers, Jungle Tortoise concluded, "The Heart's sensitive rhythm, its beat, has been disturbed by its recent uprooting and abuse. It seems to fear being touched again, and so hides itself from the men-fish." He decided that the maximum depth of the cenote needed to be sounded.

The poles, minus their gourds, were bound together and fed as one through a gap in the middle of one of the rafts. When the enlarged pole met resistance and stopped descending, a mark was made on the remaining above-water section and deducted from its total length. The depth thus calculated was found to equal the approximate height of six men. Jungle Tortoise hoped that this measurement showed the true bottom-depth and not merely the presence of a projecting rock or the peak of a submarine mount. Too, he wanted to make the subsequent search as safe as possible: the continual turning of heads and of bodies changing direction could, in a small space at depth, be dangerous for the men, and their relatively limited vision could lead to disorientation and panic. He announced that the royal brothers would now be accompanied by only five other divers, and instructed them to use a new technique: diving from his raft, each man would hold on to a rope bound to a heavy rock. This rope, in its turn, would be attached by a noose to a descending pole. The pull of the rock would guide the diver quickly to the hoped-for bottom of the cenote, and extra-long gourd poles would offer air at depth. Should a diver have problems, he could hold on tightly to his pole and jerk it to signal for it to be raised, facilitating his speedy ascent to the surface.

The brothers dove first. Twin Iguanas especially felt exhilaration at the long-forgotten sensation of water flowing over his skin. The increased depth made the pressure on their ears much more noticeable. With each descent, they had to clear the pressure, pinching and blowing into their noses, thus venting some of the precious air through their ears and into the water. The pain in their heads was dispelled but the reduced quantity of air in their lungs shortened their time below the surface. Thus, this smaller group of searchers were compelled to visit their gourds more often than in the shallows. To avoid choking should they misposition their lips when drawing air from a gourd, they used their tongues as splashboards. Even this precaution was not failsafe and sometimes a diver was forced to return to the surface for air. At the cenote's bottom, shifting patches of sunlight acted as both waxing and waning torches, intermittently revealing a brief history of the gifts offered to the cenote and its denizens: a pectoral of jade, zoomorphic ceramics, even a skull and a scattering of human bones; some of these offerings were partly covered by algae, and doubtless others had been made invisible by the sediment of time.

My senses are tingling, thought Smoke Macaw on the third dive. *I know that we are nearing the end of our search.* Then he saw it: a brightness of colour that seemed to pulse with life, animated by the sun's rays. He scooped the large shard of shell from the bottom and tapped Twin Iguanas on the shoulder. Twin Iguanas' eyes widened.

The other two shards were soon found inside an

obviously new cloth wrapping that had become separated from its nearby twine binding. *Was the bundle hurriedly, or even deliberately, tied loosely, so that it would unravel upon hitting the cenote's surface*, wondered Smoke Macaw, *or did an iconoclast of Black Stone, shielded by the cloth from the contents' burning stare of outrage, hope to destroy the Heart forever by pounding it into pieces beforehand?*

Soon after, Jungle Tortoise was holding the three pieces of shell in his hands. "Once back at Quetzal Serpent," he declared, "I will reunite the pieces and the Heart will be whole again."

Chapter 14

The Hunger of Queen Death Bat

Lady Rainbow led the way. She chose not to travel by litter; though her courageous trek from New Dawn was known and celebrated by Quetzal Serpent's citizens, she wished those accompanying her now to witness for themselves that she too, a Princess used to extreme comfort, could patiently endure the rigours of foot-travel.

Not long after reaching the bottom of the hill fronting Quetzal Serpent, Bone Drum ordered his party to start heading west instead of east.

Why are we not hurrying to my father, as I commanded? wondered Lady Rainbow. Smelling betrayal, she reached for the mahogany axe at her hip; its head was decorated with a deeply etched profile of her face, and thick, black glyphs denoting her name and rank lined the reddish-brown handle. It was a mostly ceremonial tool, but potentially lethal in determined hands. *I am in too close proximity to my enemies*, she decided, *to guarantee myself a safe escape. Too, armed conflict between Bone Drum's contingent and ours is best avoided; as is custom, the parties of guest and accompanying host are equal in number, and a victory for the palace guards of Quetzal Serpent would thus in no way be certain.*

Bone Drum announced a halt, to check that all of the party were still in single file. He noticed Lady Rainbow's eyes straying to the sides of the column, and his ensuing warning confirmed her helplessness. "If you break away," he said, the merciless look of the practised killer in his eyes, "you will be outrun by a spear."

Yes, thought Lady Rainbow, *the spear's tip of green obsidian would lodge in my head. Matching my eyes of jade, it would transform my living face into a funeral mask, my body lifeless before it hit the ground.* "Such bloody words are unbecoming from the man who once asked for a Princess's hand in marriage," she retorted out loud. *Though undeniably a prisoner*, she consoled herself, *I am at least spared a second oppression: that of tedious travel in a litter, enclosed in a privileged cage.*

Distracted by thoughts of her father, she had neglected her men, she realised; she decided to engage them in light, distracting conversation, so as to drive away any fatalism that might be settling upon them. Turning around, she saw that they were no longer behind her. She guessed that they had been discreetly removed from the column, doubtless with spear tips at their throats to guarantee their silent cooperation.

"So, you are leading me away from the path I should tread," she called ahead to Bone Drum. "Is this a blow in return, delivered upon a woman who has already warded off the intrusion of your lips?"

It was as if she had said nothing, for Bone Drum gave no reply. *We move unceasingly, like a column of ants*, thought Lady Rainbow. Suddenly, she understood. *Bone Drum, the leading ant, is taking us to the earthen mound of the Queen.* She felt something between curiosity and apprehension at being led to this female warrior, the ruler of a city state equal in power to Quetzal Serpent.

She saw tall trees lying on the ground, and trampled undergrowth; the once-mighty forest here had been humbled by human hands. Though she saw and smelt woodsmoke, she heard no human voices; only a fanfare of silence to announce their party's arrival at Black Stone. Peering intently at an unnatural-looking area of vegetation, she wondered why no light broke through the occasional gaps. *K'in's departing trick upon human eyes in the dusk*, she thought. With their spears, Bone Drum and one of his warriors parted the irregular section within the wall of green, and Lady Rainbow passed through the hanging. A gasp escaped her lips: rising up before her was something imposing and dark – close enough, she feared, to stride towards her and crush her if it wished. She stepped back. From this new perspective, she could see that she was standing not before a malignant giant, but at the base of a building with steps so steep that they resembled a wall, rising to the summit of what she now recognised as a pyramid. *Its stone is the colour of night – surely the ruler of Black Stone's homage to the bat and its time of greatest activity*, she guessed. Specks of iron pyrite on the black-painted limestone caused the structure to sparkle. She looked behind her. *The softer vegetation there must have been woven onto a sturdy frame. The wall of green, then, is in fact an enormous hedge. The plants, leaves and young vines, trimmed and shaped, enclose a living gate to the city, stunning strangers like myself as they leave an area of devastation to suddenly behold an architectural wonder.*

Lady Rainbow was led behind the pyramid. On the other side of a grassy square was a second, identical pyramid, in front of which were waiting subjects of Black Stone. A tall figure, cloaked and hooded, stepped forward from among them. Watching the faceless figure approach her, so graceful that it seemed almost to glide, Lady Rainbow wondered if it had been summoned here from the Underworld. Removing the cloak, the figure's lowered head slowly rose.

"Welcome to Black Stone, Green-Eyed Lady Rainbow," said Queen Death Bat, her eyes fixed on her unwilling visitor. "Though young and strong, you surely need a period of rest after the long journey from Quetzal Serpent. When energy has returned to you, my attendants will perfume and dress you, then bring you to my sleeping chambers."

"Your sleeping chambers?" repeated Lady Rainbow, angered by the presumption that accompanied the Queen's words of welcome. She stood tantalisingly close to her captor, within striking distance, and her left hand crossed her waist, ready to lash out. She roared. "I demand to be returned to Quetzal Serpent. You cheapen your own bejewelled blood by using trickery to entice away a King's wife-to-be, deceiving her with words whose constancy is as fleeting as dew exposed to the new day's sun."

"I wish to entertain you, and you to entertain me, during your sojourn here," replied Queen Death Bat calmly.

"However, be warned: if you do not follow my commands and fulfil my wishes, my tenderness could become venom."

Before departing, she ravished Lady Rainbow with her eyes, letting saliva ooze from her mouth. Lady Rainbow's face contorted in repulsion at the ominous lechery.

Chapter 15

The Lizard and the Dragonfly

Lady Rainbow awoke, her mental and physical numbness gone. Her first and strongest memory was of drinking continuous gulps of water to reswell her mouth and tongue, desiccated from the enforced march across the plain to Black Stone. Along that route, which had not been generous in its gifts of shady places, she had been offered no water, and had asked for none.

She recalled having been prepared for Queen Death Bat's reception. Female attendants had revitalised her, washing her body clean of the smears of travel bereft of luxury. They had then cleansed her face with a steam bowl and massaged her gently. After a light meal of fruit pieces accompanied by maize balls filled with cooked, leafy *chaya*, she had been dressed in a long lower garment of a softness and lightness she had never seen or felt before; its colour, stretch and transparency reminded her, disturbingly despite its beauty, of an ageing spider's web. Her hair, normally pulled back or coiled and pinned over her head, now served as her only upper garment: hanging straight, it partly covered her breasts.

"My time thus far at Black Stone seems so brief that I would believe my experiences here to be merely a thing of my imagination," she said to herself, "were it not for the contradicting evidence of my new vestments, and fresh perfume upon me, as heavy in scent as the forest after days of rain."

Lady Rainbow was once again at the front of a column of warriors. *Here in the subdued light of the forest*, she thought, *the whiteness of my garment stands out against our skins, like a bright pearl at one end of an unclasped, wooden necklace.* To her right, she could hear a strong flow of water, which she guessed to be the White Water. On her left was a sheer rock face; a continuous inland cliff whose height she could not gauge. She understood the significance of her present situation. The line of bodies was moving at a slow, measured pace, all heads erect and focused on the distance. *We hurried to Black Stone, but now we march only at half-speed. Clearly, I am part of a procession.*

The trail led down to a wide natural depression in the ground. At the bottom of the trail, the 'necklace' broke apart into individual beads. Lady Rainbow saw that the cliff here made a wide, concave turn before resuming its original course through the forest. A little way up the cliff's face was a large, round space; a dark mouth emerging from the rock. Seeing boulders scattered below the cave, Lady Rainbow wondered, *Are these the Earth Monster's missing teeth, lost in trying to blast out of its crushing rock prison? If so, the rise at the trail end behind us would have been the perfect dais from where to witness such a spectacle.*

Two warriors walked up the cliff face using steps cut into the rock. They lit and placed standing torches, one at either side of the cave's entrance, then returned to the depression, where Black Stone's astronomer-priest was monitoring the preparations. After a short time, a faint rumbling issued from the cave. *The innards of the Middle Realm seem agitated*, thought Lady Rainbow. The sound became louder, Lady Rainbow experiencing it as a subdued, drawn-out belch. Then it happened: leathery splinters started spewing from the mouth in the rock. She dropped to her knees and made a shield of her fists to avoid being struck in the head, but the rest of the party did not move. *They know from previous encounters that no protection is necessary*, she realised. No longer blending in with the shadows of the cave, hundreds of wings became visible, dispersing upwards in all directions. Lady Rainbow's eyes followed the endless stream and saw that high above was a large break in the varied headgear of the lordly trees; the hundreds, becoming thousands, of bats were making their nightly journey through the scattered bounty of the forest. After a night of feeding on airborne insects and on fruits found high in the trees, they would return to the cave. There they would rest, hanging by their clawed feet from the walls.

Queen Death Bat's men were looking expectantly at the cave, and Lady Rainbow also drew her attention away from the dreamlike spectacle of the bats. She felt drowsy again. At Black Stone, her goblets of water mixed with fruit juice had tasted slightly bitter – had it been the sharpness of some unripe fruit, she wondered, or had her longed-for drink betrayed her, in disguise feeding her a will-stripping narcotic? Another form emerged, indiscernible at first, from the cave mouth. A few moments later, the bodies of the squeaking bats were banking sharply with perfect timing away from the obstacle in their midst. The now clearly female human form raised her head to behold the gap in the forest canopy; her face was as serene as a mother looking fondly upon her departing children. A few more bats left the cave, individually and in small groups, until finally the tall woman stood alone.

"Now that the storm of blurred wings has passed," said Lady Rainbow to herself, "I can see that the bats' namesake has assumed a different form."

The Queen of Black Stone had green skin that bore a scaly pattern, strikingly complemented by a loincloth and a breast band of sparkling black. *The same kind of black as the her pyramids*, thought Lady Rainbow. The Queen's hair was knotted in a ball behind her head, held together with a long hairpin surmounted by a stylised forked tongue. Framed against the cave's mouth was thus a half-human, half-reptile. Her subjects were already kneeling in awe. More torches were lit, this time below the cave, and the Lizard Queen ordered a large, canopied litter to be brought up the steps and placed behind her. Next, she motioned to Lady Rainbow to also ascend, but she had to be half-carried up the steps, so weakened was she: a beggar at the mercy of her thirst, she had, in desperation, just drunk water that had also been drugged.

From the cave mouth, the astronomer-priest Nine Stars spoke. "Warriors of Black Stone, you have been chosen to witness the consumption of the graceful dragonfly by the crunching lizard. Here in the Cave of the Bats, your Queen will thus balance out the weight of humiliation dropped upon our heads at Water in Stone by Smoke Macaw and his team."

Now the Lizard Queen addressed Lady Rainbow, whose head was completing erratic orbits in the space around her. "Lady Rainbow, your dress indeed reminds me of the delicate quality of an insect's wings. Come with me to my lair; feel my wondrous skin that is in fact so much softer than the graze of a lizard's touch. Let the lizard's flicking tongue delight in the alluring fragrance of your fear; let the human part of me revel in the flattery of your fascination. I am hungry. The brittle shell of your will has been broken, and now I can feast on your inner softness, as does the hunting lizard on unhatched eggs."

Lady Rainbow offered no resistance. She let the Lizard Queen put her hand on her waist and guide her to the litter; a miniature of the typical Mayan hut of reeds and a thatched roof. Lady Rainbow toppled into the litter, its thick, folded blankets breaking her fall. She found it welcomingly spacious and comfortable, and uttered a loud sigh of relief. Her host watched her for a short while, allowing her 'guest' to relax, before joining her in the litter. Both women were kneeling. The Lizard Queen opened her lips and her extended tongue flicked from side to side as if tasting the air for food. She leaned forward, inhaled Lady Rainbow's perfume, and stared into the eyes of her prey. When she lifted her captive's hands, though only slightly, the latter in obedience raised her torso fully. Lady Rainbow trembled in confused pleasure as the twin hangings of her hair were parted and the Lizard Queen's tongue lapped, leisurely, at each breast in turn. Then she delivered light smacks of desire to Lady Rainbow's lips with her own. Finally, she pulled Lady Rainbow's mouth against hers. The women's breasts brushed rhythmically against each other as the Lizard Queen swayed from side to side. With her conflicting emotions overcome by sensory stimulation, Lady Rainbow lay back and surrendered fully.

Outside the cave, fires had been lit and the Queen's men were eating in silence. Occasionally, a loud moan could be heard from the litter, and through the thin drapes could be seen the silhouette of one woman sitting astride another. This unsettled many of the men directly exposed to the sights and sounds of the mutual pleasure taking place just above them. Like vultures waiting for the gorged predator to leave its kill, a few even hoped vaguely that the human lizard, once satiated, might let them enjoy the 'carrion'. Nine Stars sat alone. The successful completion of this night's events he viewed as assuring his future as high priest of a Mayan empire. The area was cleared of any organic debris that might appeal as a refuge for scorpions, snakes or spiders; the heat and smoke from the fires would keep away most of the mosquitoes. The sleepers took to their reed mats and guards were stationed at the foot of the cave.

Two of the sleepers were woken and escorted to the royal litter. In their turn, they woke their Queen.

"Lady Rainbow, too, has undergone a metamorphosis," she said, looking down at her still-sedated, semi-willing companion of the night. "Whereas mine demonstrates my power as ruler and demigoddess, hers is degenerative: her political status has diminished greatly overnight. She is now a mere husk of a Princess."

She drew back the hangings of the litter. The two men entered and knelt beside the sleeping woman. One opened a ceramic pot and tipped a quantity of liquid between her lips; then he and his companion opened their cloth bags and took out their tools.

The litter had been removed and the Lizard Queen and Nine Stars were standing in the mouth of the cave. Lady Rainbow lay before them on a reed mat, the nakedness of her royal body the Queen's parting insult to both her rank and Smoke Macaw's love for her.

Nine Stars addressed the torch-bearing assembly below. "At Quetzal Serpent, there was no official ceremony to make Lady Rainbow a true ruler's wife. Indeed, she has allowed herself to be pleasured by another, here in the Cave of the Bats. She is therefore now unworthy of the title of wife of the King, and its accompanying power."

Now spoke the Lizard Queen. "Smoke Macaw's diminishing reputation is an uncared-for palace: invading tree roots collapsing its masonry, unattended weeds blanketing its glory. First, the King of Quetzal Serpent unwittingly facilitated the theft of the Jaguar Heart. Then he left his chosen lady poorly guarded in his absence, leading to her kidnap and despoilation."

The warriors let out a brief, controlled roar.

The Lizard Queen turned away from all other ears to whisper to Lady Rainbow, whose now clear and attentive eyes had broken through the post-narcotic mist still paralysing her limbs. "This night is to be chiselled upon my monuments. Never have I tasted such beauty; never have I drunk and eaten of the human form with such urgency. But even as you rest in delicious exhaustion, do not forget this: I will remain a part of you forever. You need not blacken your tongue with words of shame when Smoke Macaw finds you, for I have left him an indelible record of our mutual history. Your illicit time with me, woman to woman instead of woman to man, will accompany you unceasingly, as surely as a shadow follows its caster."

Somewhere between sleep and waking, Lady Rainbow's ears registered the squeaking of bats. Her eyes opened slowly in response. She remained awhile, lying on the reed mat, half-consciously taking in the dimensions of the cave walls and ceiling, allowing isolated memories from the night before to drift back to her. Recalling what had happened in the Queen's litter, she wished she could snap off one of the stalactites hanging far above and use it to pierce Queen Death Bat between the breasts. Suddenly fully awake with anger, Lady Rainbow's body registered the hardness of the cave floor that penetrated the mat. The combined coolness of the cave and the early morning made her shiver. On the damp, sticky floor next to her lay her white lower garment; its purity also compromised. Though she now found it as unappealing as a cloth rag, she reached out and drew it over her, to cover her nakedness.

The bats were beginning to return to their cave. As she rose from the ground, Lady Rainbow refused to flinch at their speed and proximity, for she did not believe that they intended her harm; nor did she wish to grant them any special consideration – Queen Death Bat was their ally, not she. Areas of her arms and legs felt sore; intuitively, she checked her skin for ceremonial cuts. And indeed, as if bats had somehow collided with her sleeping figure, on the outer side of each upper arm and each upper and lower leg was a tattoo of a bat head and wings. *So, this is the legacy of my half-remembered night with the Queen of Black Stone*, she thought. *This is what Smoke Macaw's eyes will be confronted with. What will he feel; how will he react? Is it possible that his love for me will prove to be a shallow brook that disappears in a drought of disappointment?*

On the cave steps, she noticed a cape of grey fox fur; no doubt dropped from the royal litter as it was carried back down to the clearing. She draped it around her shoulders, revelling in the warmth it provided. Back down among the scattered boulders, she looked up at the cave and wondered if other events had taken place that night. "Did the Earth Monster, its former prison now its lair, see what happened in the Queen's litter, or was it sleeping deeply in the dark of the cliff's interior?" she asked herself finally. "If it was a witness to my desecration at the Lizard Queen's flowing hands and relentless lips, what did it decide: to accept my ruin with indifference, or to right the crime committed against me and mete out punishment to my violator?" She waited, continuing to gaze at the cave mouth, hoping for an answer. None came. Looking around her, she saw no sign of carnage; of justice dispensed. Concerns about Smoke Macaw, her father and her own future vied for her attention, her fleeting thoughts like leaves caught up in a whirlwind inside her head. Her confusion held her in place, as if she were a bas-relief figure carved on a stela, unable to step out of its frame.

When the rising sun burst into sight through the foliage, she felt her lower limbs begin to move again, as if of an independent will, leading her out of the forest.

"As I now return to my adopted city," she said, "perhaps Smoke Macaw and I shall meet along the way, drawn together by the guiding forces of our spirit doubles. Such a blessing I would honour with a bountiful offering of fruit and flowers upon the temple summit at Quetzal Serpent."

Chapter 16

Two Life-Drums: A Pact

Lady Rainbow was from the openness of the coast, and so she found the almost continual shade of the forest oppressive. The thought of breaking back out into unfiltered sunlight gave her new strength. The sparser the vegetation became, the less tangled her mind; she saw that she was leaving the domain of the Cave of the Bats, that area of forest fed by moisture from low clouds meeting the high, rugged escarpment.

She entered the shyer green of the plain, where no river flowed. As the heat of the morning sun began to drive the cold from her body, her numbness of spirit, the haunting after-effects of last night's surreal events, also ebbed away. From the surrounding stunted trees she saw emerge half of a human form. *As when a human and an enchanting creature of the forest chance upon each other on a narrow path, so am I here halted in happy surprise*, she thought. *His hitherto hiddenness makes me think once again of the quiet, camouflaged brocket deer; and, like it, he emanates caution, for he remains at a distance, looking behind and around me. I cannot be offended by his tense posture, for surely he trusts me; rather, his behaviour displays the instinct of the warrior and the wisdom of the ruler, of one who is ready to meet possible danger but who does not act hastily.*

Forsaking his woody cover, Smoke Macaw walked slowly towards her. Lady Rainbow wondered if she was not being visited by a mere memory of him; a moment from her past taking form to comfort her in this time of doubt. *I hope that my imagination is not painting an illusion in the air before me; that what I see is no trick of the heat rising from the ground, but the real Smoke Macaw, waiting for my hands to touch him with love.*

He was now close enough to her to detect the subtle uncertainty in her face, accentuated by a dank staleness that seemed to cling to her skin. "Lady Rainbow," he said, "when I heard that you had gone as you had come – unannounced – even Quetzal Serpent's ball game victory near Water in Stone could not console me. I feared that my next and final encounter with you might present me with only a beautiful corpse upon a funeral litter. Escorted by one such as Bone Drum, why did you leave with only the palace guards? Despite protocol, a full contingent of warriors could have been arranged to go with you. We were preparing to leave Water in Stone when the runner-messenger Rain God on the Wind informed us that you were no longer travelling in the direction promised you: towards New Dawn to be with your father." He paused and looked her up and down, appreciating afresh her loveliness. He made to draw up next to her. Then he noticed her scars – the bat tattoos – and froze.

"Smoke Macaw, my disfigurement is a record of last night," she explained, "and you must see beyond the simpler message presented to you. My spirit double had also been kidnapped, preventing me" – here she took a long breath – "from offering any resistance to… the warrior Queen's touches."

Smoke Macaw recoiled, as if struck by an unseen adversary.

"In my weakened and drugged state, I confess I experienced some of her attentions as pleasurable. But now the traces of her caresses are a hornet's sting inflaming my skin. Look into my eyes, Smoke Macaw, look down into a clear sea of truth, where insincerity can only drown. Be assured of this: you are the one I wished was near me when I woke again, my thoughts and actions once again truly of my own uncompromised will."

Smoke Macaw's face, initially rigid with shock, softened at the openness of Lady Rainbow's words. He put his arms gently on her shoulders and brought his eyes close to hers; so close that she thought their lashes would touch. "You and I remain two that are one, Lady Rainbow. Our togetherness is as a perfectly formed seashell, whose twin lobes may not be prised apart to rip out that coveted pearl – our love – as a trophy to the revenge of Bone Drum and the ambition of Queen Death Bat."

She gripped his topknot and guided his lips to hers. The juice of his mouth was more satisfying to her than the freshest mountain rainwater. She held his cheeks in her hands. "Bone Drum told me a story to be sure that my emotions won out against my reason. He made me believe my father's skin, bones and blood to be ready to leave this world, and so I hoped that my earthly journey would take me to him before he commenced his deathly one. Once under way, I discovered that truth was not our guide, that we were following a path of lies, but I could do nothing; my palace guards had dissolved like smoke in the wind."

"Lady Rainbow," Smoke Macaw reassured her, "these scars chiselled upon your body were intended to disrupt your glorious destiny. Instead, they mark the beginning of the end of Queen Death Bat's rise to power. She has scorched a royal bastion, but we will transform this attempt at destruction into a thing of rare beauty. The violence wrought upon the Princess of New Dawn makes her no less worthy of the King of Quetzal Serpent; if anything, it makes her yet more loved."

He kissed her, a long kiss, and they embraced awhile.

Smoke Macaw continued. "I believe Queen Death Bat is holding your guards as barter for a later time, as movable stars should the greater political constellation prove to not be aligned to her advantage. We know that she and Bone Drum are allies, but what can be your father's position in all of this? Does he not feel at least moderate envy upon hearing of other cities' achievements; do not the arms of his mind reach out acquisitively upon learning of their possessions?"

"The blood of my father and his people pulses in time with the coastal tides and winds," answered Lady Rainbow. "The gently undulating sea we do not fear; as a child each person learns to swim and to enter the blue world below. Only the Great Storm do we fear; shelter from the anger of the salty waters we find in the nearby forest, where we also plant and hunt. Like all Maya, we grow maize. Ours has a special quality, however: its stalks being short, it is hidden from view behind high grass, within small, natural forest glades. This is our best defence against any would-be invader – perhaps wearing the mask of a trader to New Dawn: our plots being hidden and scattered, they cannot easily be found and burned to starve us into submission. We also accept gratefully what the sea offers us: fish of the reefs and the deeper waters, the long water-squash that sleeps on the seabed, and the gaping-mouthed, tapering ribbon snake that lurks in the underwater rocks. All these good things we have, and we know we have enough. As my father has often said to me, 'A full stomach that devours ever more is sure to burst, the contents spewed out visible testimony to the glutton's greed.' My ancestors built high walls around New Dawn to defend our city against raiders. This, and the enemy-swallowing sea Great Blue Water remain our initial protection. We have a sister city – though, so much smaller than New Dawn, it better resembles a settlement – called Eastern Rock, that lies on an island of the same name.

"To finally soothe the ache of your curiosity, Smoke Macaw, my answer is: no, we do not actively seek prestige, though wealth finds us in the form of trade with the Putún Maya. I know my father; his moods are unlike the sea winds, that change direction often. We can be sure that banishment by King Parrotfish from the whole territory around New Dawn will be Bone Drum's reward for aiding Queen Death Bat in kidnapping a King's daughter. My father wishes for three things: a bloodless peace among the Maya; continued, modest trade; and a married daughter."

Smoke Macaw was contented. He was certain that he would have an unshakeable ally in King Parrotfish, and thus friendly relations between their respective cities. Too, and he shared this thought with Lady Rainbow, "You are a caressing breeze from the coast, come to cool me of the weighty heat of rule. In you I will have a Queen who will delight my nobles with accounts of life above and below the sea, bringing bright colours into the sometimes-monochrome court life of Quetzal Serpent."

He could see that the fox cape had kept her overly warm, for her neck and shoulders had a moist glow to them. Slowly, he removed the cape. Her breasts now exposed, Lady Rainbow drew in her breath. Smoke Macaw wanted to feel her warmth, her heartbeat. He lowered his head and she drew him to her, whereupon he laid his face against her breast, "To feel and absorb the rhythm of your life-drum," he whispered. She felt a faster ebb and flow inside herself of the coastal tides she had spoken of. After a time, he arose, his eyes aglow and an expression of deep relaxation upon his face. First brushing off with her hand the dust from his chest, she dribbled saliva upon his left nipple, then licked the area clean. Now she shared of his heartbeat.

Lady Rainbow was the first to voice what they were feeling. "Even a priest experienced in sacrifice would be unable to sever our spirits now that they are merged."

"Yes, my life, it is true," confirmed Smoke Macaw. "Should I ever find myself bound on foreign temple steps and forced to confront the *tok*, the sacrificial knife, I would in that moment remember that your heart, twin to my own, resonates in harmony with mine. Secure at least in the fastness of your love, I could accept with contentment my fate, awaiting then our eventual reunion in the afterlife." Embracing her from behind, his arms became her new upper garment, his hands covering and holding her breasts. "Tomorrow we will continue your broken journey to your father. Twin Iguanas and Jungle Tortoise are in charge of Quetzal Serpent until I return alone."

"Return alone," she repeated thoughtfully. "You are right, Smoke Macaw: I must remain with my father. Your place at this time is with your people."

"Sadly," he confirmed, "tonight will be our last together until it is judged safe for you to leave the protection of your father's city. But it is late, and we should hang our sleeping nets between the trees."

Looking around, Lady Rainbow could see no equipment or provisions. However, she decided to ignore the improbability of Smoke Macaw's present situation: a King alone here in the wilderness, unarmed save for a hipknife. "What of the clinging jaws of Crocodile Lake, the most direct route to New Dawn from here?" she asked, her creeping thoughts of sleep displaced by this great puzzle. "How will we reach the other side of that lake, inhabited as it is by monsters as terrible as any mentioned in the Mayan prehistories?"

"That is indeed worth considering," he replied. "How to pass by the hungry meat-eaters of the sweet waters, and yet be ignored by them? The new K'in will cast the light of knowledge upon you, when I hope also to enjoy your look of surprise in revelation."

Lady Rainbow laughed. "I suspect a collaborator in this riddle of yours, Smoke Macaw. If Jungle Tortoise were here, I would ask him the answer, though before answering, perhaps he too would allow himself the pleasure of watching my thoughts take form as guesses dancing across my face."

Smoke Macaw smiled in agreement. Facing the area of vegetation from where he had appeared, he whistled. Warriors of Quetzal Serpent appeared from behind the seemingly deserted bushes and trees. In a semicircle formation, they all dropped to one knee, steadying themselves with their spears.

Lady Rainbow stood close to Smoke Macaw. As all the warriors had their eyes on the ground, she took the opportunity to whisper to him, "Now I have the answer to an earlier question. Even in the dizziness of love, no one, be they maize-gatherer or King, could risk coming here totally alone. Your men were waiting patiently for your signal."

"Yes," he answered. "Silent like the occasional rocks to be found here, they were alert, but respectful and unobtrusive. They had instructions to listen carefully for any discordant sounds of struggle or pain – but also to look away from our simple altar of soil and bush, to guarantee our royal privacy. Not all ceremonies are meant to be witnessed by other human eyes, and our pact of hearts was deeply personal. The sky and the sun, manifestations of K'in, were our unofficial priests, and the creatures of the wild our Middle Realm witnesses."

Smoke Macaw placed his left hand in Lady Rainbow's right. Raising their joined hands high, he addressed his men. "Warriors of Quetzal Serpent, we rejoice at the safe return of Lady Rainbow. Show now that you will follow her commands as you follow mine. For, just as an individual head emerges from each end of the Sacred Serpent's body, so are Smoke Macaw and Lady Rainbow two beings become one. Confirm your allegiance to my future wife, to your future Queen."

Lady Rainbow was surprised at the grace with which the warriors unfolded their crouching bodies as they rose. Spears were raised, accompanied by one voice that was strong but not warlike: a tone of commitment.

Chapter 17

Crocodile Lake

The search for Lady Rainbow had prolonged the stay on the plain for Smoke Macaw's party, consuming prematurely most of their torches, and the materials here were not suitable for making replacements. Thus, the morning meal – a mash of maize flour mixed with cold water and a little chilli powder – was eaten perfunctorily in near-darkness. Lady Rainbow could see that Smoke Macaw was impatient and guessed that the difficulty of quickly breaking camp by the predawn light was stealing yet more time from the party; time they would need, she guessed, for an early crossing of Crocodile Lake, when its eponymous denizens would be sleeping.

The party resumed its trek, describing a curve in the general direction of the lake and the coast. Smoke Macaw travelled on foot behind his litter, which was occupied by Lady Rainbow, standing in order to view the route ahead when daylight awoke. She had only travelled here once before, but her present lack of sure orientation through experience would later be compensated by her ability to smell the salt water on the coastal air.

It was still dark when the landscape changed. The appearance of reeds told the party that they were now at the shore of the lake. In the presence of water, the air was cooler, and smelt of decaying plant matter. Lady Rainbow's litter was placed on the surface of the lake. *The purpose-built rafts at the cenote functioned well enough*, thought Smoke Macaw, *but this makeshift one might not be of the right form or light enough to be buoyed by the water here.*

His concern proved unfounded, however, for the litter indeed became a raft, submerging only slightly. Smoke Macaw marvelled again at Jungle Tortoise's knowledge of matter, and simultaneously wondered at his priest's earnest piousness. On one occasion, sensing Smoke Macaw's struggle to reconcile this apparent paradox, Jungle Tortoise had reassured him, "I see no contradiction in an empirical knowledge of the world around me and a continued belief in the gods. Must I deny all the traditions of the Mayan cosmological order simply because I understand some of its principles? As I learn by analytical observation, so is my respect strengthened for the divine, creative forces that are the source of what we see and experience."

Staying close to the litter-raft, Smoke Macaw's men waded slowly into the water and prodded its surface with spears, testing for submerged crocodiles. Lady Rainbow was given a long staff. She too probed the water and found it to be waist-deep. She began to punt to the rhythm of the men pushing from the rear of the newly fashioned watercraft. *Though unwieldy*, she thought, *this staff might be of use in an encounter with one of the powerful creatures; the silhouettes of which I see lying on the nearby bend in the shore. Are they sleeping, or patiently relishing the possibility of fresh meat, with which we tempt them as we traverse their world?* Their bodies were surprisingly flat, distended along their flanks – "Hopefully, they are already bloated after gorging on fish," murmured Lady Rainbow. Smoke Macaw later said that perhaps this was true, but added that, on land and no longer supported by the water, this predator always lost some of its sharpness of form.

Smoke Macaw whispered to the men nearest him. "This message is to be relayed to the whole party. We must move quickly, for these now slow creatures will not long remain so. If the water reaches our shoulders, the less experienced swimmers may hold on to the raft, still swimming with one hand and pushing with the other. The stronger swimmers can follow in a compact group. When the lake becomes shallow, we will halt the raft and rest. Remember, a quiet crossing will less disturb the crocodiles' rest, so give hand signals when possible. Remain together; do not become a fish that has lost its shoal. If it pleases the deities above and below us, the crocodiles will decide that we are one giant turtle crossing the lake: Lady Rainbow and the royal raft its head and carapace, and the groups of individuals around the raft its flippers and tail."

The raft again shifted a little below the surface as Smoke Macaw boarded and stood up next to Lady Rainbow. "This raft is carrying you," he said quietly, "the beloved of King Smoke Macaw, across unknown waters, a Xibalba of the Middle Realm. Now I will share my secret with you; the answer to the question that I have, more than once, seen tantalise your curiosity since we left the safety of the lake's shore."

"Yes," she said, "end the light torture inflicted upon me. I must know."

"The crocodiles' blood is cold after the long night," explained Smoke Macaw, "thus they are presently sluggish. However, K'in's shafts of light will soon fall – ever more in number as the day unfolds – upon their bodies, jabbing them back to life. It is only for the first part of the morning that we will move without the company of meat-hungry eyes and stomachs. Nonetheless, we may be fortunate in our crossing in that a crocodile rarely attacks a creature it perceives as much larger than itself."

Lady Rainbow was unable to suppress her laughter, albeit light, at Smoke Macaw's explanation of the riddle he had set her. Then she said, "I become all the more curious to know better Jungle Tortoise, who is not only diviner and royal adviser, but also intimate knower of the non-human."

The light of the moon on her face reflects her inner contentment, thought Smoke Macaw. With a smile, he recalled Jungle Tortoise's foretelling in his *Book of Prophecies* of the appearance at Quetzal Serpent of a Princess of the sea – Lady Rainbow, he now realised – during the cycle that coincided with Smoke Macaw's reign.

He observed the log-like, legged forms scattered along the lake shore. Illuminated now – for the Disc of Time had freed itself of the bondage of the horizon – he saw that the crocodiles' previously shadowed skins showed barred highlights of green. Alternately eyeing his course ahead and watching for signs of rippling or disturbed water to his sides, Smoke Macaw lightly clambered down from the raft back into the water, and moved to its front. The water had shallowed to standing depth. Leaning forward, he and several men proceeded to pull the raft, each with a rope harnessed at his chest and shoulders; at the rear of the raft, others pushed in unison. Lady Rainbow resumed punting, alternating from left to right as she pushed the pole into the lake bed. Earlier, Smoke Macaw had wondered whether it might not be unseemly for a woman of high rank to perform such physically demanding and potentially dangerous work, despite her famed courage. His misgivings left him when he recalled the humble appearance of his father, his body a random pattern of scratches and chalk dust, as he built with the stonemasons the new city of Quetzal Serpent. Like Jaguar Phallus, Smoke Macaw believed that, beyond royal commands to obedience, inspiring speeches followed by visible examples from the ruler were the best way to catalyse one's subjects into action. The ruler's subsequent declarations of satisfaction with the efforts of his subjects should guarantee their continued loyalty. "It is the ruler's actions that bind into a firm knot the disparate political elements of a city state," he often reminded his nobles. Regrettably, public displays of punishment were occasionally necessary too, when that knot showed signs of unravelling, loosened by the ambitions of high-ranking individuals or by unjustified aggression towards other city states.

Smoke Macaw was proud of his rule thus far, not least because he had managed to limit the size of Quetzal Serpent's nobility. Leading up to the Great Decline, Mayan society had been weakened by the nobles' lust for luxury. In Jungle Tortoise's words, "Their activities had, like destructive beetles, left holes bored throughout a once-healthy *yaxche* tree; roots, trunk and crown – like the distinct layers of tilled soil, huts, and lofty temple complexes of a city – had become a rotten thing that was doomed to collapse from within." For this reason, in Quetzal Serpent high social status had to be maintained by performing regular acts of service: male nobles accompanied hunting expeditions and stood guard over the city at night; their female counterparts assigned tasks to the maize-gatherers and craftsmen, and watched the marketplace for dishonest transactions. Thus, each noble actively contributed to the city state's well-being.

Years before, Smoke Macaw had even suggested to Jungle Tortoise that membership of the nobility should cease to be a birthright; that only acts of true distinction should be rewarded with the title. "To heal any wounds of disappointment or humiliation," he had said to his priest, "those deemed by us as inappropriate to enter the nobility could be publicly praised for other achievements and then found new, non-noble functions to fulfil."

Jungle Tortoise had sympathised with Smoke Macaw's idea; the youthful King wanted to prevent a situation in which there might, one day, be more nobles than their city state could support – "more nobles than maize-gatherers", as was sometimes humorously remarked, in derision of other Mayan communities. However, he had countered that "Any system of personal merit alone has its limits in actual harmony of governance. Once some have been seen to ascend the revered stone steps to heady privilege, many of those destined to spend their lives on unprestigious low ground will feel resentment towards their ruler." A fever of competition for rank had in the past infected multiple city states. Thus, Jungle Tortoise had advised, it was better to keep to the existing system, wherein high rank was not lost but had to perpetuate itself through acts of direct participation in the daily life of the city.

The lake remained shallow and the party passed miniature islands. Lady Rainbow could now see crocodiles of various sizes, half-hidden among the sand and the grass. The larger ones were about the size of a man and had broad snouts. The smaller ones – their young, she guessed – had flanks striped with half-finished, vertical black bands, and their darkish upper bodies were flecked with yellow points. Struck by the colours and patterns, Lady Rainbow forgot her punting and steering, and recalled the Mayan flood myth:

It was the Moment of Creation. For the planets to be set in motion, a sacrifice of enormous scale would be necessary; Sky Crocodile was beheaded. From his severed neck flowed jade and turquoise beads, shells of spondylus and conch and glyphs of magical spells, all this flooding the sky and earth. The glyphs spoke by themselves, creating the first dawn. The sun rose, the moon lit the darkness and the gods scattered the stars across the sky.

The new Mayan cosmos had just been created, in the year Ahau 8 Umcu (3114 BC).

A flock of large herons, their long, smoky-blue bodies and their yellow-white bills clearly visible as they flew past, suddenly brought Lady Rainbow out of her reverie, the noise of beating wings a rattle to wake her. She also sensed her name being 'called': Smoke Macaw's eyes were scolding her, albeit mildly. Without her punting, it had become noticeably harder for the men in front of and behind the raft to propel it through the water. Smoke Macaw held up his hand in a halting gesture, to give his men the impression that the raft's slowing was his wish, and not due to Lady Rainbow's inattentiveness. He reboarded and gave a long, low, warbling whistle, to deceive the crocodiles into believing that they heard a bird of the lake, not a human.

When she was sure that all the party were looking up at the raft, Lady Rainbow followed Smoke Macaw's mime to her: she held up her gourd, put it to her lips and drank, gesturing to her subjects-to-be to do likewise. They did so without hesitation. On the steps of their temple, they had seen Lady Rainbow willingly shed her blood for them, for their King and for the Great Ancestor Founder. They had voiced their allegiance to her the day before. Her commands, now and future, were to be heard as echoes of Smoke Macaw's wishes, spoken or unspoken. The pushers and pullers of the raft exchanged places; their lord's strategy was for them to rest certain muscles and now use others. With Smoke Macaw choosing to swim ahead, the journey was resumed. The men spat out the slightly salty water that occasionally breached their lips, fearing that it was poisonous; by contrast, Lady Rainbow's nostrils twitched in greeting to the nearby sea, though the haze in front of her blocked any view of it. From time to time, a long object approached the raft and closer observation revealed a pair of eyes and a back-ridge resembling tree bark: a crocodile. The party were no longer near the lake shore and, at the present depth, escape from an attack by one of these creatures would be a challenge for the lithest warrior. *Even I*, thought Smoke Macaw, *though a quick mover through water and a semi-divine ruler, would not be able to outswim one of these descendants of Sky Crocodile.*

"Smoke Macaw, we are entering the territory of New Dawn," called out Lady Rainbow, in her excitement forgetting his admonition to discretion when vocalising here.

He appeared not to notice her transgression, however; saying nothing, but simply boarding the raft to share her view of the scene ahead. The haze had been burned by the sun; from up here they could see how the lake reeds thinned out, to be replaced by the tidal lagoon's mangrove trees that formed a permeable border with the sea. Still wary of changes in the crocodiles' behaviour after basking in the energising sun, Smoke Macaw slid very slowly into the water once more, his eyes darting all around him. Unexpectedly, his feet just touched the bottom. Again, he swam ahead of the raft, confident that, in such shallow water, he could quickly rejoin the party should Lady Rainbow whistle a warning of danger. It seemed, however, that the presence of humans – as if at times born of the 'giant turtle', then mysteriously re-merging with it – had not whetted the crocodiles' appetite.

The water grew shallower still and Lady Rainbow saw below her a small stingray: its round, flat, dazzlingly white body with bright yellow spatters stood out against the relative darkness of the sandy lake bed. It was with the spine of a stingray that she had pierced her tongue in the ritual at Quetzal Serpent; thus, she took this encounter with the whole, living creature as another sign of approval of her bloodletting, that her visit to her father would be a happy one, and that both New Dawn and Quetzal Serpent would prosper in the future. The stingray moved away from the advancing raft, the sides of its body undulating to propel it slightly upwards and forwards before it settled again on the lake bottom. Its body then shuddered, stirring up the sand, which rose and fell again to cover the stingray, leaving exposed only its hole-like eyes and its spine.

Lady Rainbow broke the silence, this time with confident, full awareness. "Men of Quetzal Serpent, you are about to enter a world different to any you have seen before. New Dawn is the gateway to permanently deeper water; home of the large-headed, many-armed creature whose colour changes to match the underwater rocks; and where the underwater flowers are as bright as any to be found on land. Sometimes leaping from the water with a smile is a large fish that, like a human, must breathe air, and that forms groups to race our speeding canoes. These are some of the marvels that you may encounter during your visit here."

Chapter 18

The Oracle

A party of King Parrotfish's men canoed the deliverers of his daughter back to the inland end of the lake. The return crossing was faster and, without the necessity of immersion in water, virtually without risk of attack by the lake's largest predators.

Smoke Macaw sat at the front of the lead canoe, close to the guiding paddler. The repetitive sound of the paddle slicing through water cut deep. "The constant alarm of loud water in my ears is as a watchful companion," he murmured, "warning my thoughts not to drift too far." The position and sequence of approaching and receding landscapes, often obscured during the outward crossing, he was now committing to memory, should he need to travel here again. Once satisfied that he knew the route from Crocodile Lake to New Dawn, he allowed his inner eye to recall the various images he had collected of that coastal city. "New Dawn is a fitting name," he judged, "for the city faces the eastern horizon. Too, as the sun is each morning reborn, so have King Parrotfish and his original subjects recreated themselves. They fled the inland chaos of the Great Decline and found refuge among the few people still inhabiting this lonely old city, promising both groups a new beginning."

The royal and ceremonial centre of New Dawn was protected on one side by Great Blue Water,[2] and on the other three sides by high walls. Only one narrow passage through each wall gave access to the city proper – a similar concept to the killing alleys at Quetzal Serpent. The buildings of New Dawn, however, were crudely cut and, compared to those of Smoke Macaw's own city, appeared unnaturally low and cramped, as if built not for human habitation but for the dwarf-men of Mayan legend. Perhaps, guessed Smoke Macaw, even the palace and temple complex here were more symbolic than practical.

Greater New Dawn – the area outside the walls and the clifftops beyond – seemed dilapidated and partly deserted. Smoke Macaw knew that the population was not large, and so reasoned that the city probably had neither skilled stonemasons nor strong bodies enough to chisel stelae or lift myriad blocks of limestone. Moreover, few of the buildings showed signs of having been painted; unusual in a Mayan city. Some of their decorative elements, however, spoke of dedication to New Dawn, its inhabitants and its deities. Engraved in niches on some temple walls was a simple, inverted humanoid form, its arms and legs spread out to the sides as it seemingly fell from the sky and into the sea. This was the Diving God, the patron of underwater fishermen. On

---

2   The Caribbean Sea.

one two-level temple, King Parrotfish had proudly showed Smoke Macaw a rare mural depicting his daughter swimming among coral and accompanied by various creatures of the sea – was she the human counterpart to the Diving God, Smoke Macaw had wondered?

One night, from the beach below New Dawn, King Parrotfish and some of his court had canoed the visitors from Quetzal Serpent out to sea. The party included, Smoke Macaw noticed, Lady Yellow Knot. She was Lady Rainbow's sister and had earlier been introduced to Smoke Macaw. The sisters were facially unalike: Lady Yellow Knot's face was slender, not broad. Her hairline was set far back on her scalp, the eponymous yellow knot holding her hair in place. Her large, expressive eyes had seemed to search Smoke Macaw's before she finally turned and walked away to talk to a group of nobles. *So far, Lady Rainbow has not left my side*, thought Smoke Macaw. *Later, however, just as King Parrotfish and I will take the time to clarify our political relationship, so will the sisters, once alone together, surely exchange news and share their hopes. Perhaps then the meaning of Lady Yellow Knot's as yet mysterious glances in my direction will become clear.*

The paddling stopped. The five canoes grouped in a circle and long torches were leaned out of them at an angle, the flames turning the water to liquid fire. A knobbed stick was rubbed at short intervals along the side of the royal canoe to produce vibrations. *A summons to something still not visible*, thought Smoke Macaw. The action was repeated. The only response came from the breeze: it became stronger, causing the torch flames to flicker and reducing the artificial illumination of the water, as if the thing – or things – summoned wished not to be seen. After a while, the sea air breathed more slowly again. Smoke Macaw thought he saw movements below the surface; indistinct but purposeful. Oversized wooden bowls of a runny, stinking substance were poured into the water near his canoe. Smoke Macaw recognised animal entrails and large pieces of fish offal floating on the water's surface, which was now tinted orange. The movements, now closer to the surface, became more regular in frequency.

Upon King Parrotfish's command, two men lowered themselves into the water. They initially held on to their canoes, treading water. Lady Rainbow then motioned to Smoke Macaw to follow her as she too entered the water. As she guided him in, he thought, *Perhaps she is indeed a goddess of the sea, about to draw me down into some salty Xibalba.* His concern was all too obvious and Lady Rainbow made to conceal her amusement, but Smoke Macaw's eyes were faster, easily outpacing her strategic movement of hand hiding mouth. Two long poles were placed against the side of a canoe, each to lean at an angle to the water. At the end of each pole, tied with cord, was a large mahi-mahi (fish with tapering body and deeply sloping forehead), still struggling with desperate life. Hung by their tails close above the sea's surface, they were dipped regularly into the water, allowing them to continue breathing; the dips were timed to coincide with the passing of the forms below the surface. The forms started to move as a pair. They drew closer to the group of bobbing canoes, following the demarcation in the water created by the stationary flotilla. The men in the water were now swimming, and Smoke Macaw saw that each held a short shaft of wood, noosed loosely to the wrist via a cord. *Is this all a prelude to our wedding ceremony*, he asked himself, *wherein I demonstrate to New Dawn my courage in the face of the unknown?* He silently thanked Jungle Tortoise for having encouraged him and Twin Iguanas to spend time at Open Sky Cenote when they were children. He noticed the greater ease, compared with those boyhood experiences, of remaining suspended in this water. Jungle Tortoise would later explain to him that salt water was more buoyant than fresh water.

Smoke Macaw and Lady Rainbow watched the swimmers complete the canoe circuit three times. She reminded him of the number's significance. "See how we honour the Mayan hearth fire, here symbolised by the reflection of the torch flames on the water. The original hearth, presented by the gods to the first Maya, still has three border stones of flint."

Slowly, one of the forms in the water took shape, and a part of it breached the surface to reveal a greyish, tapering appendage that stood erect from the middle of a silver-coloured back.

"A stepless pyramid built upon the temple body of a water-breathing deity," said Smoke Macaw aloud. "The fearsome soup thrown into the water, and the two hanging fish, must therefore be offerings."

Both the observers and the swimmers had a hope, steeped in awe and fear, to see next the head; as breath-robbing as any visage portrayed in the wood, stone or plaster of the Maya peoples' arts. A second, almost identical 'pyramid' became visible, rising above the water. Smoke Macaw wondered if the pair might be marine manifestations of the Heroic Twins of mythology. Certainly, he had seen the two brothers portrayed as aquatic beings before: as carp, at inland Mayan locations. King Parrotfish, if asked, would have confirmed his guess.

One of the swimmers yelled briefly, then felt for the wholeness of his leg: he was inadvertently swimming through the lure of blood and flesh. He found, to his relief, that he had merely been bumped into from below. Being one of those nobles who disdained the low-born fishermen, and having a distaste for their sea, the young man remained nervous; his high-born pride barely controlled his mean panic as he swam quickly away from the potential attack. He did not know that the deity in question occasionally grazed a fisherman in the water, to see if he shed blood and might thus be suitable prey.

Parrotfish gave a hard, short blow on a conch shell. The swimmers returned to the hulls of their canoes and trod water again. Lady Rainbow did not follow them, but swam towards the centre of the enclosed water, pulling on Smoke Macaw's hand. Despite his earlier confidence – "The individual fish, when part of a large shoal, loses its fear of a predator," she had informed him – he again felt uneasy, for now they were alone in the water and he did not know if the deities flitting around them were benevolent or not. It briefly occurred to him that he might even be an unwitting sacrifice; the mahi-mahi only a minor lure to a much greater reward.

Gazing over at her father's canoe, Lady Rainbow seemed unaware now of Smoke Macaw, who in his turn momentarily forgot the alien beings so close to him. Her face was only partly turned towards him; thus his obviously critical eyes were not directly in her line of vision. He used the opportunity presented by her distraction to study her face, tracing his mind's fingers over her features. His portrait finished, he relaxed anew: beneath the perfect surface of her face there was no substrate of trickery to be found, and he felt ashamed. His suspicion of her was unworthy of the King of Quetzal Serpent, and an unvoiced affront to the Princess of

New Dawn; had they not, in each other's presence, sworn a pact of hearts? Had not her father welcomed him with both regal respect and a warmth normally reserved for family and close friends?

More than once, as they swam together Lady Rainbow felt Smoke Macaw's hand squeeze hers gently. *I should have known from the moment we entered the water*, he thought, *that my trust in Lady Rainbow would prove its worth: the deities have not approached or struck us.* He remembered the murals at New Dawn, depicting Lady Rainbow swimming among coral. This was not merely the flattering fantasy of a royally commissioned artist, for here Smoke Macaw saw that she was indeed equally at home in this underwater world; if she had met these twin deities before, it would explain her lack of concern in their presence now. As he again admired the now less threatening symmetry of curving angles that passed before them, he recalled Jungle Tortoise's admonition to constant objectivity and self-questioning: "See also with eyes that are not your own." Thus, Smoke Macaw understood the duality of what he was witnessing. *As deities*, he thought, *they officially receive King Smoke Macaw; yet the animal part of them relishes the prospect of biting off chunks of the seductively hanging fish. Too, our party may seem to the deities a curious thing, transported here as we are upon a form of uncertain origin, lacking true fins or tail, that does not swim through the water but glides across its surface, not unlike the flying fish I saw earlier today.*

At her signal, Lady Rainbow and Smoke Macaw stopped swimming. At the gunwale of King Parrotfish's canoe, their hands and wrists linked up with those that then pulled them out of the water. Once back on the canoe, they were given double-layered cloaks to dry their skin and to shield them from the breeze.

Smoke Macaw's eyes had grown accustomed to the contrast of burning torch and darkish water, the constant change in ratio depending on the whim of the breeze and its effects on the torches' powers of illumination. He could see that the marine deities were moving slowly, just below the water's surface, and so close to the canoe that they were almost touching it. Only now could he fully appreciate their extreme proportions. Each part of them was long: the supporting, angular black-tipped wings on the sides of the streamlined, powerful body; the forked tail, the upper of its two prongs noticeably longer than the lower. The sharp-edged limbs resembled knives. "Knives…" Smoke Macaw repeated to himself. Inspired by his utterance of the word, he answered his own earlier question: the pieces of wood borne by the swimmers were probably clubs, to be used as deflectors should one of these hunters of the sea attack. The panicking noble had apparently forgotten about his club, or had not dared to use it; looking again at his face, Smoke Macaw noticed that his expression of concern had become one of veneration, for now he was back in a familiar element, and buoyed by wood, which he knew would not succumb to his weight and return him to the water.

The deities moved away from the canoe and began again to swim back and forth, now at greater speed, through the chummed water. The suspended mahi-mahi were dunked in the sea and withdrawn with increasing frequency. The process was repeated several times but still the deities kept a distance from the captive prey, waiting to be caught with virtually no effort.

"Though predators, they are cautious," Lady Rainbow told Smoke Macaw, "always weighing any risks against the potential gains of their actions before launching themselves upon a target. Now, however, hungry or not, their hunting instinct has been stimulated fully."

King Parrotfish held out his hands towards the sea and slowly opened them. He began to chant in a monotone, using many words that Smoke Macaw did not recognise. The Mayan language spoken at New Dawn struck Smoke Macaw as simple; *possibly an archaic form*, he theorised, *unchanged in perhaps centuries, due to the city's isolated location. Moreover, King Parrotfish might at this moment be using specific words to refer to the coast and sea which are therefore unknown to us inland Maya.*

The mahi-mahi seemed to know that their lives would soon be ended and absorbed into that of another being. They jerked furiously on the vine lines and flipped up their broadly tapering bodies, the bright blue of their steeply sloping heads clearly visible, their flanks the colour of Jungle Tortoise's silver mirror, and their undersides as if splashed deep yellow by the sun. After a while, one of them stopped moving; this, and the fading of its previously striking colours, were a confirmation to all of its death – from combined exhaustion and lack of water-breathing, Smoke Macaw presumed. A paddler pulled back into the canoe the pole holding the lifeless fish, and cut the securing vine. With both hands, he skilfully hurled the heavy fish, its body skimming across the surface of the water as if new life had come to it. A brief eruption of water stopped its passage. The fish disappeared, removed from the surface by a greyish body much larger than itself. The acceptance of the sacrifice continued. From the opposite direction, a second head emerged, exposing first a broad, rounded snout and then a mouth filled with multiple blades of white. Smoke Macaw wondered if the expressionless eyes were watching not only the mahi-mahi but also him, the honoured stranger to these waters; in his turn, he looked into those black orbs that shone in the light of the torches above them. The second mahi-mahi's twisting, thrashing movements snapped the deliberately weakened vine cords, but its leap to freedom was short-lived.

"The open-mouthed deity effortlessly enters that space between sea and sky," murmured Smoke Macaw.

Serrated teeth clamped down on the fish, both creatures then hitting the water with a slap. The water frothed briefly, then closed over both predator and prey. The last whisper of doubt in Smoke Macaw's mind was silenced: he had just witnessed the deathly beauty of the "top hunter of the sea" that Lady Rainbow had mentioned; the aquatic counterpart to the jaguar on land.

"Just as the Diving God is protector of the fishermen," she explained now, "so is Xoc the protector of the creatures of the sea. We believe that an attack by Xoc on a human is punishment for our having overexploited the hunting and harvesting grounds below the waters. The powers of the Diving God and Xoc create a balance between the needs of humankind and the wholeness of the non-human world: the sea."

Indeed, in addition to the Diving God, Smoke Macaw recalled having seen at New Dawn carvings of a second being: a featureless, humanoid face with a single large tooth, and two fins on its back: the deity Xoc, he now realised. "Jungle Tortoise has spoken to me before of opposing yet complementary forces similar to your two deities," he replied. "He calls it 'creative tension', as when two city states understand that to conduct raids or wage war on each other could lead to the destruction of both of them. So arises a political stability that has its origins in mutual caution. Constant vigil and reassessment of the situation are necessary, however, as this peaceful status is of little depth. The two city states are as a giant tree with a double trunk sprouting from a single base. The shallow roots offer only a fragile stability; nonetheless, they are widely and evenly spread, like the relative contentedness of the citizens, and so the whole remains strong. Yet, should the simultaneous storms of internal popular unrest and external military aggression roar through the forest, the life of even a holy *yaxche* can come to a premature end, ripping its own roots out of the thin soil as it topples towards the forest floor, its growth rings a mere whisper to future generations of its former greatness."

Parrotfish turned to Smoke Macaw. "King of Quetzal Serpent, you have this night shown your worthiness of my daughter's love. You have trusted her to guide you through waters of a nature immeasurably different to those of any cenote. You have swum in the presence of Xoc, the shark deity of our waters. Manifesting today as a pair, with ties to the Heroic Twins, Xoc has acknowledged your worthiness as King, accepting you in his waters without attack."

He then took hold of Lady Rainbow's hands. "Daughter, your return has brought the air back to my suffocating lungs. I no longer need wander our city in my sleep, like a thing half alive, seeking your spirit double, longing for succour in memories of you as I revisit your favourite abodes. To know you gone again will bring me pain, but this will be replaced by a massaging comfort: once you and Smoke Macaw have launched your shared canoe upon the open sea of married life, the strength of your love for each other will enable you to navigate together the bewildering currents and countercurrents met on this oft-unpredictable odyssey; to ride over any waves of crisis. Should gods or men conspire against you and indeed capsize you, your craft will always be righted once more."

Father and daughter looked into each other's eyes. Sadness gave way to happiness.

"Smile not later, but now, Father," she replied, "for I will berth my own canoe next to yours awhile. I will keep anchorage here, in the safe harbour of your paternal love."

"Yes, venerated father of Green-Eyed Lady Rainbow, beloved daughter of New Dawn," confirmed Smoke Macaw. "King Smoke Macaw and his wife-to-be can be truly reunited only when this chapter of their life story has been written to its rightful end; when our nostrils must no longer strain at the stench of the Death Bat's vile breath, that menacing blast of wind, as if from Xibalba itself, that threatens to sully the peaceful air of Quetzal Serpent and New Dawn."

Parrotfish nodded. "By returning Lady Rainbow to me, Smoke Macaw," he continued, "you have replaced the oppressive silence in the chambers of my head with the contentment of easy laughter."

Too, thought Smoke Macaw, *Lady Rainbow is now far removed from the risk of vindictiveness on the part of her scorned suitor Bone Drum, or a repeated mauling by Queen Death Bat.*

Lady Rainbow's unannounced departure had been

devastating to New Dawn's morale; too, the Sacred Calendar's count of years since her mother's abdication as co-ruler and subsequent emigration had been too short to exert the moonlike pull of forgetfulness upon her subjects. Now it was as if the count had been erroneous and subsequently adjusted, and New Dawn was healed of the wounds of its loss.

Parrotfish raised his hands and addressed all present, speaking loudly against the breeze. "A temple or palace is only as strong as its foundations. Let our two city states be the first tiers of solidity upon which a new, non-destructive Mayan world may be built. Let the joining of Lady Rainbow and King Smoke Macaw initiate the inseparable and prosperous futures not only of New Dawn and Quetzal Serpent, but of all Mayan city states."

Led by Parrotfish, the occupants of the five canoes chanted, "King Parrotfish and Xoc. Lady Rainbow and King Smoke Macaw. New Dawn and Quetzal Serpent."

Age honoured youth, Parrotfish resting his arms on Smoke Macaw's shoulders, looking down slightly in humble thanks. He then placed his daughter's hand in Smoke Macaw's, finally clasping them in his own. Neither of the young royals had needed to formally request his consent to their marriage; he had seen their longing for each other, and this linking of their hands was his official answer. A public display of affection was required by protocol. So far at New Dawn, Smoke Macaw and Lady Rainbow had been able to share only occasional affectionate glances. Impatient emotions had strained long enough against the bonds of dignity, but now the cramping cords had been officially severed by King Parrotfish's liberating words, and the two promised ones could express themselves more freely. The vitality of their embrace and kiss was eloquent of their feelings for each other. For those around them, the enamoureds' passion was palpable, like moist, charged air before a storm. Against a background of political threats and physical danger, the impulses and hopes of their hushed love had seemed to them little more than a vaguely glimpsed constellation in the night sky of their shared lives. Now, in the benign presence of King Parrotfish and his subjects, this publicly sanctioned approval of their union reassured them that they had a fixed point of emotional reference, an axis of certainty that, like the Milky Way, held unshakeably in place their own stars.

The supernatural rabbit-scribe would later portray their kiss in a folding book, using quills from the mythical bird Muan to record for eternity the events of this night. On the sacred tree-bark paper would be painted the two young royal heads in profile, their lips interlocking. The emblematic glyphs for Quetzal Serpent and New Dawn would appear directly above the depiction, rendering the kiss a symbol of this pivotal moment in the common history of the two city states.

Chapter 19

The Drinking Vessel: An Empty Promise, Richly Embellished

In her palace, Queen Death Bat lay on her sleeping-frame, stretching and wallowing in anticipation. Beneath the thickly woven blankets, bound firmly to the wooden frame, three layers of palm-leaf latticework reacted with delicate spring to the shifting form atop them. Her head, dizzy from the alcohol she had drunk with her nobles, was comforted by cushions filled with the buoying seed-fluff from the silk kapok tree. She smiled: her body and mind were already in a state of intense relaxation, and soon the aches of her desire and her loneliness would also be soothed.

Though her senses were half-numbed, she clearly heard the sound: something stopping abruptly outside the entrance to the chamber. The hanging beads at the entrance parted, as if by a gust of wind. A sweeping arm, then a face, appeared in the doorway and finally revealed itself to be the full form of a man. The man gazed at the Queen's half-closed eyes and open lips. Moving around her naked, reclining body, his eyes flitted from one irresistible source of pleasure to the next: arousal's wings hovered awhile above her breasts, then settled on the centre of her, where surely fragrant forest gave way to a well of delights. Her eyes opened wider, the better to appraise his features. His face seemed made of weathered brown stone: his jawline had a chiselled hardness to it, and his pockmarked complexion was almost unhealthy in its appearance. His frown, as well as the lines around his squinting eyes, made him seem older than he was. On the face of such a man, the line down one cheek could only be a battle scar, she decided; a spontaneous tattoo earned when bodies and weapons had clashed, that moment in his past slashed deeply and permanently into his skin.

Queen Death Bat raised herself slightly on her elbow and looked hard into his eyes. She was momentarily disappointed. *His sense of protocol is poor*, she thought, *to enter a Queen's chambers without a courtly greeting; and his attire, only a simple loincloth, is hardly that in which to be received by one's new ruler.* Nonetheless, she found his rough-hewn features and his powerful chest attractive. Too, she was flattered by the sympathies he apparently shared with her: his threatening visage could almost be that of a god of Xibalba, and she was the incarnation of the terrible Death Bat. Thus, she quickly forgave his shortcomings and gazed with approving curiosity at the ring of curving, serrated teeth hung around his neck.

She rose from her sleeping-frame and held up a ceremonial drinking vessel. "Bone Drum, let us drink to our future victory."

The Queen was first to drink; a formality to demonstrate that the offering was not drugged or poisoned. She then handed Bone Drum the vessel and he too drank greedily; the hot, fermented chocolate, flavoured with vanilla, was considered an aphrodisiac.

"Now that both your lips and mine have touched it," she informed him, "this vessel holds within it the pledge of Queen Death Bat and Bone Drum to vanquish Quetzal Serpent."

Despite the liberal use of bright Maya blue on the vessel's surface, Bone Drum did not notice the scene it depicted: the profile of Queen Death Bat, and suspended before her in defeat an inverted human head with a scar along the side of its face. On the other side of the vessel was an inscription: 'The Ephemeral Ally.' That he might look at the artwork closely made, for her, their meeting an exciting game of chance – and if her prediction regarding his inattentiveness to detail proved wrong, she would remain nonetheless the winner, being herself an outstanding warrior and her guest outnumbered by yet more of them. She smiled again. She had guessed correctly that Bone Drum was too lacking in reverence to take any great interest in the artwork of a ceremonial vessel; too, she doubted that a coarse warrior from a half-forgotten city could even read glyphs. *Alliances come and go, just as lives begin and end*, she reminded herself silently. Almost tenderly, she placed the vessel on a shelf.

She looked Bone Drum up and down expectantly as she approached him. The warrior's mouth was open; he could feel the heat of her sexuality. Both of them were impatient to fully consummate their alliance. Their standing bodies touched. She grasped his hanging hair and, coiling it around her hand and forearm, jerked him to her. She smothered his lips with her own and pushed her tongue into his mouth; when she finally drew back to breathe, both of them had chocolate-smeared lips. Bone Drum pushed Queen Death Bat back onto her blankets, where she managed to land in a seated position. From under a cushion she revealed, with exaggerated slowness, a penis sheath of extremely thin, finely brushed fawn skin. Precisely applied tree resin made the sheath leakproof; the Queen was not yet ready to commence her dynasty of female rulers. In any case, her breeding partner would be another: Smoke Macaw, her equal in rank. This night, however, she intended to explore fully the extent of this warrior's strength and endurance; the sleeping-frame now their battlefield.

The captive energy in Bone Drum's loins had by now become visible beneath his minimal loincloth.

"Your male limb promises to match in bulk that of the bearded tapir," she complimented him. "Let me relieve you of your pleasurable discomfort." She leaned forward to undo the restricting loincloth.

Chapter 20

As Fast as Rain on the Wind

Chac Ik[3] detected a change beneath his feet: the dry, solid soil was becoming slightly springy, moistened by the water that penetrated it. He had arrived at Crocodile Lake.

Removing his small, body-contoured, high-strapped backpack, he took out one of the two slim water gourds and drank. He sighed as the still-cool water quenched the dryness of his mouth and then trickled slowly down his throat. Though his name was known to all in his home city and beyond, he remained humbly aware of the smaller blessings in life and was always grateful for the immediate return of energy bestowed upon him by a few measured draughts of this most divine of liquids.

Not for the first time, he found himself mildly surprised by how long he had been travelling, and with how few rest

---

3 'Rain God on the Wind'.

stops. Modest self-acknowledgement quickly changed to a warming sense of pride. *My present achievement indeed befits the wind of my name.* He had set out from Quetzal Serpent at sunrise. The specially toughened leather of his clothing offered exceptional protection. His running-sandals, cushioned with inlays of felt and reinforced at the heel, the ball of the foot and the toes, were comfortable yet sturdy. On his lower legs he wore chaps, for rattlesnakes were a danger on the plain at this time of year. His torso was protected by a slim-fitting, three-layered tunic, the intermediate layer a light lattice padding of split cane. Around his head was bound a cloth band, and over this he wore a helmet of light wood, worked to depict the visage of Chac, the rain god of this dry, riverless region. The god's hooked, downward-curving nose partially protected Chac Ik's exposed lower face. Small seashells embedded in the helmet recreated Chac's square-framed eyes. The human eyes within were barely visible, the skin around them darkened with charcoal to minimise the intensity of the sun's reflected glare. The helmet's relatively loose fit allowed some air to circulate and cool the wearer's head and face, which might otherwise cook in their own juice of sweat.

If a message was not urgent, Chac Ik preferred to run by night, when the air was cooler and human attackers slept. He considered it a benediction of the gods when the celestial torch – the moon goddess U – travelled above him to illuminate the ground, enabling him to travel at almost daylight speed.

Though encounters with people were rare on this deserted part of the plain, he had once encountered a group of dishevelled men – social outcasts, he had guessed – not far from Quetzal Serpent Hill. Encircled by them, even his agility had not prevented him from being hit by a large stone hurled at him, but his helmet had proved its worth, the wood and cloth absorbing the impact with ease. Apart from a bruise on his exposed skin, he had evaded further injury or capture by running directly towards the two men blocking his escape route, dodging past them, and finally breaking thorough the enemy line. Once in flight, he had used his standard technique of sprinting over short distances while frequently changing direction, swerving to alternate sides; this confusing pattern of unpredictable movements made him a virtually unassailable receding target.

Even as a young boy, this son of maize-growers had distinguished himself by weaving effortlessly between seed-planting sticks hurled at him by his playmates. A group of nobles checking maize yields had witnessed this and reported it to Smoke Macaw, who had then summoned the boy to his palace court to display this unique skill. Training with Twin Iguanas, the boy had perfected his style of mobile self-defence. His final test had been to evade the spears – only partially blunted – of Smoke Macaw's best throwers. Now the official messenger for Quetzal Serpent, his instinctive sense of danger approaching from behind had earned him the popular name of 'Double-Headed, Four-Eyed Chac'. His other allies were endurance and the element of surprise: beholding this god of the region unannounced, hurrying to an unnamed destination, initially robbed potential assailants of decisive action. Should anyone be reckless enough to attack at extreme close range this manifestation of the rain god Chac, however, the assailant risked the ultimate punishment: death. Chac Ik's one weapon was an obsidian longknife, its face edged with a double blade. Carried on the back, it could easily be unsheathed from behind the shoulder.

Chac Ik turned to face Crocodile Lake once more. He sat down on a rock, to recall the events so far and to plan the next stage of his journey. His King had left Quetzal Serpent with no idea of Lady Rainbow's whereabouts, and so no clear time frame to adhere to. A tower sentry at the high plateau drop-off had later seen, coming from the plain below, coded signals sent from a disc of polished silver; another of Jungle Tortoise's applications. The sequence of flashes combined with slow beams – which could be single or double – reported that Smoke Macaw and his search party had found Lady Rainbow and were travelling across Crocodile Lake to New Dawn, to remain there for some days. But collective relief's initial sigh soon became the shallow breath of concern when a trading party visiting Quetzal Serpent one day later reported having seen canoes at sea, heading in the direction of New Dawn. Their passengers could have been traders or warriors; the witnesses had been too far away to discern details. It would take half a day to organise a precautionary war party plus provisions, so Jungle Tortoise had sent Chac Ik to warn Smoke Macaw of the possibility of an attack. It was planned that warriors from Quetzal Serpent would arrive at New Dawn close upon the heels of the messenger.

"By Jungle Tortoise's reckoning," said Chac Ik to himself, "the party should pass by this part of the lake sometime between now and sunrise. When I see the canoe torchlights, I will call out to them."

He remained seated, letting his eyes adjust to the darkness that was now filling the air around him. Twin Iguanas had often spoken to him in the courtly language of metaphors, and now Chac Ik considered his own situation abstractly.

"This rock, this coarsely wrought throne for an unwilling occupant," he said. "I, lord of emptiness, with no obvious kingdom nor visible subjects to rule over."

Then he thought of the near future. He imagined how the people of Quetzal Serpent would welcome his return, and celebrate his completed mission and great service to their lord. How would his life be thereafter, he wondered?

Later, to keep awake his gradually slumping body, he periodically left the rock. Walking a short distance away and back, he swung his arms and stretched his body by reaching up to the sky. As Jungle Tortoise had warned him after entrusting him with the royal message, "Rest gives new life, but to a man readied for action, extended inactivity is an enemy as dangerous as any weapon." He kept restlessness and boredom at bay for as long as he could. He tried to think back to his childhood, but the memories escaped him. His resolve to keep his mind busy was weakening, his efforts becoming a drain on his creativity; he was exhausting his strategies for adapting to the unaccustomed decelerated speed of time here, time that passed no faster than the observed passage of the stars across the sky. He felt more and more the frustration of waiting, unrewarded, for his king's arrival. Finally, he began to feel overwhelmed, the blanket of sleep drawing inexorably over his heavy eyes.

Chac Ik was woken not by the daylight, but by the almost human whistling of the great-tailed grackle of the blackbird family. Smoke Macaw's party was not to be seen.

"I have to make a decision," Chac Ik said. "Either I wait

longer for the possible appearance of my king, or I continue alone and deliver the message directly to New Dawn."

A more mundane consideration – the ache in his posterior from the hours seated on the rock – prompted his decision. As he rose, he noticed a movement among some reeds a few strides from the shore. *Could it be a crocodile?* he wondered. If so, the tricoloured heron in the shallows did not seem concerned about the predator's presence; nor did the red-throated, shinily green-breasted hummingbirds feeding from the pink flowers. Chac Ik stood on the rock for an elevated view of the scene. Even from here, the tall, secretive reeds only reluctantly offered him glimpses of the object. As a composite, however, these glimpses formed something recognisable. *A canoe*, he realised. *It must be held in place between the reeds and the clumps of vegetation that form where the land meets the water. Perhaps it has been abandoned, being too worn to be of further use.*

He stepped down from the rock, impatient to learn more about the man-made thing that seemed grossly out of place in this wilderness. Unremittingly cautious of snakes, only when right at the water's edge did he take off his shin pads and sandals, and place them alongside his helmet on a mound of grass. As he neared the canoe, the heron waded further out into the lake. *As wary of me as of any nearby crocodile*, Chac Ik guessed. The heron was acting wisely, he thought, for of all the creatures in the Middle Realm, the human was the most gifted in cunning and in variety of movements – and thus the most successful of hunters. Swim fast and deep enough, and the fish might escape the diving cormorant; the launching wings of a keel-billed toucan could save it from the lunge of a tree-prowling ocelot; the human, however, though handicapped without fins or wings, had nets to hem in fleeing fish and slingshots to kill birds already in the air.

Chac Ik was immediately struck by the canoe's simplicity of design. It was a dugout, carved from a single tree. The hull bore many scars from an adze, testimony to workmanship of minimal skill, and the sides, the gunwales, were noticeably irregular in height and evenness. Slowly, he leaned forward and peered deeply into the canoe. His action, though unthreatening, triggered a streak of movement. He looked behind him, and smiled: the blur of blue-and-yellow stripes – the flanks – and orange – the digits – had now coalesced on a nearby reed, and he saw that he had just inadvertently disturbed a red-eyed tree frog. The heron, the hummingbird, the frog: this variety of colours cheered him after the night, its blackness relieved only by white specks, the renewed presence of other creatures driving away his loneliness.

He returned his attention to the canoe. Pieces of downy pollen and fallen reed stalk littered the inside, no doubt creating convenient bedding for various non-human occupants. The raised squatting-blocks had acquired a green sheen of algae, highlighted by the morning dew. In some places, there were also large bird droppings – from the heron he had seen, perhaps? From all this, he decided that the canoe had been sitting there unused for some days. His eyes chancing to rest on one of the squatting-blocks, he saw that some glyphs had been chiselled there. Privileged among the illiterate maize-gatherers, he had, from his time at Smoke Macaw's court, gained some knowledge of reading and writing. Thus, he was able to guess that he was looking at a name glyph; perhaps that of the canoe's last owner. The glyphs that he could interpret referred to the sky and to a colour – blue or green; the words were often interchangeable. Roughly depicted, too, was the face of a woman. Taken together, the name would be something like 'Blue-Green Sky Lady'. He puzzled over whether this person was known to him.

Just as he felt the vagueness of the words starting to take on a clearer meaning, he was distracted by the appearance of something long, lain on its side inside the canoe. "A paddle!" he exclaimed in amused surprise. "I did not see it, made as it is of the same material as the canoe. Even now, it seems to melt into the background of its vessel. The glyphs and the careful placement of the paddle suggest that this canoe was not simply abandoned. Perhaps its paddler meant to return?"

Standing on one of the squatting-blocks, he rocked the canoe and found that it resisted him more than he had expected, indicating that it had weight and stability. He got out of the canoe and pushed it a little deeper into the water, all the while watching for ripples or for movement at the shore – he had no companions to help him should a crocodile seize him. With the water up as far as his chest, he felt with his hands under the gunwale and found that the canoe's draught was relatively deep. It could well be a seagoing canoe – beyond Crocodile Lake was the salty Great Blue Water. He pulled the canoe back to the shore and let his feet dry in the sun. Then he removed the accumulated litter from the canoe, retrieved his shoes, shin pads and helmet, and clambered back in. Once again, he felt his being transformed as he donned the Chac helmet. He pushed against the bank with the paddle, relaunching this serendipitous vessel that would bring him to New Dawn sooner than he had anticipated.

Chapter 21

A Constellation in the Forest

The lead guide of the reconnaissance-cum-war party carried on his back a tall construction of wicker, itself a bearer of pieces of vegetation. Under the bulk of the wicker frame, only the top of the man's head and his lower legs were visible, giving the impression to the men behind him of an erect, anthropomorphic turtle or tortoise. Points of white on his 'carapace' appeared then disappeared again into the darkness, and a vague rattling sound could be heard whenever his movements became strenuous or uneven. The sources of light changed position, creating different patterns on their carrier's back. Tiny, shifting stars – self-illuminating lighting-beetles – guided the party along the night-time forest trails. Others of the beetles' kind had been pierced non-fatally through the thorax and were worn as twinkling anklets by the warriors following their human guides.

"We Maya have long used these beetles to light up the interior of our night-covered huts," reflected Jungle Tortoise.

"Similarly, these tiny beings are now serving the function of discreet torches."

The beetles' organic, normally stationary home had become mobile, with sections of bushes now forming part of the travelling backrack. Every fifth member of the party, in fact, was a guide and wore such a backrack, though smaller than the leader's.

This period of tension between the city states and settlements, of secret plans discovered, and even of betrayal, counselled maximum silence when travelling, and overly bulky appendages could brush noisily against hanging branches or narrow tunnels of vegetation. Quetzal Serpent's watchtower men had seen night-time campfires on the low plain. The forms gathered in the glow of these fires were almost certainly Queen Death Bat's men; a contingent waiting to hinder any war party that might descend Watchtower Hill to warn Kings Smoke Macaw and Parrotfish of possible approaching danger, or to actually fight on the side of New Dawn in the event of an attack.

The party here was using a less obvious but also less convenient route, and at night: down the Rattlesnake Trail and then taking the fork leading away from the Black Stone Trail. The landscape in this area was hilly and irregular, and from either side of the main fork it was easy to mistakenly follow a promisingly wide trail that later thinned into a sheer wall of rock. The people of Quetzal Serpent believed, from finding bodies on the rocks below, that a supernatural guardian wind waited to blow trespassers off slippery or already crumbling cliff trails. The White Water river was fast and tortuous at this point, and the myriad narrow canyons made travel by canoe unthinkable to anyone.

As if commanded by the newborn sun, most of the beetles had stopped glowing. It was time to shed the backracks. The lead guide's bush cuttings were unbound from his backrack, which was then placed at the side of the trail. Then the other guides were freed by their companions of their happy burdens, without which their night-time journey would have required the much less subtle use of full-sized torches. All the sections of bush were returned to the forest. A few of the living anklets had worked loose or been inadvertently torn off during the journey, but the majority could now be reunited with their fellows. Following the lead guide's example, the party remained a short while, gazing in silent respect upon the beetles and their miniature world; it was a custom of Quetzal Serpent to give thanks, without pomp, to the non-human world when it had been of exceptional service.

The lead guide was a short distance ahead of his party, and thus the first to leave the forest. As nocturnal vanguard, bereft of illumination in front of him, he had acquired some of the night vision of an owl. Now, encountering the rising sun, his eyes recoiled, no longer accustomed to unfiltered light. He turned to face again the opening to the forest trail. In this comfortable space between bright sunlight and shadowy forest, his eyes slowly regained their sharpness. His ears seemed to him as sensitive as those of an ant on the ground: he heard the sound and felt the rhythm of approaching footfalls becoming louder and louder. The first of the warriors exited the forest. He bowed deeply when he saw his shaman-priest, who had led him and his companions unerringly through a tunnel of near-blackness. Jungle Tortoise studied the warrior carefully, gauging the man's physical and psychic state. He did the same with each member of the party leaving the trail, simultaneously counting off the number of warriors. Once all were gathered around him, he announced that the backracks would be used to fuel the morning fire, the warmth and maize cakes sweetened with honey the long-awaited reward for their non-stop nocturnal journey.

The river had become wider and straighter, its previous anger calmed by freedom from the confining, funnelling rocks upstream. The party followed a small tributary to a lagoon dominated by low crags and trees dangling their limbs into the water. The lagoon was in fact a large, open cenote, its original subterranean form eroded and reshaped by time, finally permitting vegetation to crowd the remains of its walls. Seawater had permeated the porous rock underground, travelling inland and gradually losing its salinity along the way, collecting in pockets of rock like this one. Though also 'sweet water', the colour and consistency of the cenote water were different from those of the turbid river, which had its origins in the mountains. This was a place that Jungle Tortoise knew well, and he always felt a deep sense of peace here. The formations of nature, not the orderly and (as he considered them) sterile constructions of humankind, were his true home. Even Quetzal Serpent's unusually liberal, relaxed atmosphere could not tame his longing to be back in the non-human realm, where the uncontaminated air and the sight and sounds of so many different forms of life stimulated his senses. After each sojourn here of a few days, he would return, contented, to his king's city, ready once again to perform his priestly duties.

"You have eaten and drunk; you may now refresh yourselves in the shallows," announced Jungle Tortoise. "If you are not one of Quetzal Serpent's swimmers, simply enjoy the sensation of suspending yourself briefly on the water's surface; identify yourself with a torpid, half-sunken crocodile waiting to rise from the water, revitalised by K'in."

Many of the men looked uncertainly at each other – normally, only their king and a few privileged individuals were permitted to enter this cenote area.

Noticing their reaction, Jungle Tortoise added, "King Smoke Macaw will again be proud of his warriors, of this war party, when he hears of the unfaltering steps of our successful first night-time traverse of the Quetzal Serpent–White Water Trail, reaching Open Sky Cenote. In your King's name, I bid you unburden your bodies and minds in the soothing water of the cenote."

Reassured now that they had not misheard or misinterpreted Jungle Tortoise's words, the previous doubters, and all others, bowed to their priest; to be allowed to bathe here was an unprecedented honour. Cautiously, the men began to partake of their gift, encouraged silently by Jungle Tortoise, who motioned them with mock impatience to the water's edge. Those who could stay afloat and propel themselves through water – a skill acquired from their challenging experience in the waters of Water In Stone – waded into the cenote and swam; others clung to surface-breaking rocks – once soaring stalagmites – as they dangled their legs in the water; and some of the non-swimmers, hoping that they would be able to stay afloat simply by moving rapidly through the water, elicited chuckles from their companions at their subsequent panic as the water failed to support their ungraceful, thrashing bodies.

The men's aches seeped away from them into the water, its

cool touch also a salve to the scraped skin incurred through carrying the hurriedly worked backracks. Temporarily forgetting the import of their mission, the warriors became carefree children at play. They barely took notice of the sobering presence of the guards stationed at regular intervals around the lagoon. Though unlikely in this remote place, the possibility of ambush could not be disregarded. At this moment, an attack upon the half-armed war party would promise an easy victory, hemming them inside the cenote area, with little room for manoeuvre. For Jungle Tortoise, however, the guards' presence was merely a display of caution; he trusted his intuition, which sensed no danger on this morning. The roles of bather and guard were exchanged, every man thus able to experience this sacred place in his own way.

The water was still and clear and reflected the surrounding crags and trees; a visual temptation to the bathers to lose themselves in a twin but less substantial world. Some indeed allowed themselves to wallow too deeply in the sensual forgetfulness of the water. Those who either did not hear or simply did not heed quickly enough the War Chief's command to relieve the guard received a mild spear-prod to the buttocks upon leaving the water.

When again dry and fully attired, the men found that Jungle Tortoise had another surprise for them. He led them behind some bushes, then proceeded alone to a large mound of upright, desiccated palm fronds lain over each other at an angle. The fronds gave way a little as he ascended the mound with no more apparent effort than that expended by the local orange-and-black striped caterpillar, often to be seen crawling up a tree in a group. Reaching the top of the mound, he began to peel away the frond covering, his deliberate unhurriedness creating in his audience a greater sense of suspense. He was gratified to hear curious whispers, and could guess the words: "What can lie under these fronds; a thing of so little value as to be left here in the open, and yet important enough to be hidden?" Finally was revealed a low structure of two racks and a roof. Upon the racks were placed eight long canoes. The men's response was as Jungle Tortoise had hoped: their faces showed surprise, then understanding, and finally relief. For those now selected to travel at speed, the rest of the journey would not be a monotonous march across land.

"It was wise to invert the canoes before storage," said Jungle Tortoise to himself. "Having collected no trickle-down water, they have not become makeshift bromeliads (spiny-leaved plant of the pineapple family), offering tiny pools to be occupied by opportunistic amphibians or aquatic insects."

The canoes were taken down from the racks and the storage structure re-covered with the fronds. The canoes were then borne to the riverbank, where Jungle Tortoise addressed the men. "We do not know if the party travelling from Black Stone to New Dawn merely wish to conduct talks or trade, or if they plan war; but if need be, we are ready to defend King Parrotfish and his city. We assume that the messenger Chac Ik has warned the twin coastal cities of the possible approach of Queen Death Bat, and that King Smoke Macaw has also had time to prepare himself. These canoes will bring us swiftly to the island of Eastern Rock, where Lady Rainbow should be residing. We suspect that, at some time in the near future, it is Queen Death Bat's intention to capture or kill Lady Rainbow."

In symbolic protection of their Queen-to-be, the warriors angled their spears upwards, their tips meeting and forming a necklace of blades. Once again lowered, they were thrust forward, shadow-killing in advance any potential kidnapper or assassin.

Chapter 22

The Messenger

During his crossing of the lake, Chac Ik saw only birds and a bulky grey creature with a flat, whiskered nose – a manatee – that breached the water's surface near his canoe and stared at him briefly before submerging again. The lake became unnavigably shallow, and so, like its previous user, he left the canoe berthed at the lake shore, choosing not to drag it to the sea. *The sea is not known to me, and am I not rather a runner than a paddler?*

The reeds of the lake disappeared, to be replaced by the woody, interlocking stems of mangrove trees, signalling the end of the sea's tolerance of its shoreline dilution into brackish water by the lake's fresh water. Through the seemingly impenetrable mangroves Chac Ik found a corridor, a route devoid of water at this time due to low tide; this had also made shallow the lake, connected as it was to the sea. He had not been in such a landscape before, and so was not aware of his fortunate timing in arriving when he did. Along the mudflats separating the mangroves from the sea, he ran barefoot in long strides, his beloved running sandals in his hands, safe from stains and discolouration.

After some time, he felt and heard that even his practised steps were being held down by the moist, sucking ground. *The contours of my feet are making me unstable on the muddy sand*, he thought. *The flatness of my sandal soles might ensure a more even landing and a stronger subsequent spring from the ground. As combat demands sweat and sometimes blood, so must I sacrifice some of the beauty of my unique footwear, designed by Jungle Tortoise and inscribed with a dedication by my trainer, Twin Iguanas.* Donning the sandals, he found that the ground still slowed him down slightly, the mud's surface continuing to part beneath him. Experimenting with his pace and his stride, he finally developed a technique he felt comfortable with: using shorter, faster strides, he was able to run unhindered, his shoes leaving the mud before its sensitive surface had time to truly register his weight. Happy with this success, he experienced no fatigue, even following effort over time. He felt only the exhilaration he always felt when seemingly moving as fast as the wind.

His environment began to change again: to the human eye almost imperceptible in its movement, the sea was nearing him. Chac Ik was surprised at this, for he had maintained the same distance to the mangroves. "So, the sea is creeping up on me," he said. "If I am not to be trapped between it and the tangled forms of those bush-trees, I must move faster." Upon increasing his speed, the extra impact of his steps drove his clad feet into the ground somewhat, again slowing his progress. Moving closer to the mangroves, he found this higher ground drier and easier to run on, unburdening his feet and legs.

Later, reducing his speed a little, the better to watch and gauge the sea's relentless rise, the runner-messenger declared, "My journey to New Dawn is as running a gauntlet: escaping one challenge or danger, I am confronted by another." Premature death on land was something he could accept, but he had a fear of dying in this unknown place of miniature forest, soft ground and tidal water. He could not swim, and he imagined how the mangroves might entangle him, make him a prisoner, forced to watch as the sea slowly water-buried him alive. More troubling was the thought that this would mean he would fail to deliver the message of state to his king: after his patient night-time vigil at the lake shore, his subsequent successful crossing, and the long run over shifting mudflats, he might ultimately never relate the story of his journey, his limp, water-softened body instead becoming a delicate meal for the crabs and mudskippers that now fled from him.

A long, wide stretch of beach extended inland to cliffs. Chac Ik stopped moving. He had left the region of mangroves and mudflats. "I know New Dawn is situated on cliffs above a beach, and I have been travelling for nearly two days. I will see people before this day's end," he assured himself. "By virtue of the veneration accorded Chac, I must trust that no arms will be taken up against me. If compelled to flee, I know that my body can dart as fast as a swallow, leaving the missiles of suspicion and disrespect to pierce only the air around me." He again tried running barefoot and found that the sand was dry and firm, so he accelerated, keeping his gaze upon the distance. "I believe that, here near the end of my journey, the god Chac and the spirits of nature are rewarding my efforts," he said, "for the running conditions are now ideal: the sea has spread evenly for me this sand I run on. How long ago seems the Great Plain's obstacle course of tripping stones and entrapping roots!"

He exulted in the breeze that dried the perspiration on his body; the cleansing air seemed to puts wings on his feet. It was late afternoon and the sea was retreating. The sun was in his eyes, causing him to squint. He blinked to clear his vision, to confirm what he thought he saw: anthropoid forms emerging from a cluster of palm trees near the cliffs. The group spread out in a line before him. Chac Ik heeded the visual command to stop. He donned his shoes once more and started to walk slowly towards the human fence. He stopped when he judged that he was approximately a spear's throw from the men, although their faces did not show the tension or the aggression that preceded armed combat.

One of the men – his bulky headgear adorned with feathers indicating high rank – called out to him. "We could not see you, we had no message of a visit, and yet we knew you were coming."

"The gods of New Dawn must be powerful, to have bestowed this prescience upon their priests," called back Chac Ik.

"This is true," responded the man, "and we know of a King who has an equally great shaman-priest, with a brotherly knowledge of the wild animals, and who explains the mysteries of life by direct experiment."

"That King is Smoke Macaw and his priest is Jungle Tortoise," confirmed the newcomer, acknowledging the compliment with a bowed head. "I am their messenger, Chac Ik, He Who is as Fast as Rain on the Wind."

"Then welcome, Chac Ik. King Parrotfish is waiting to receive you."

Chac Ik did not react immediately. "A sand grain of caution holds back my steps," he murmured. "To be sure of this speaker's sincerity, I must listen again to the intonation in his voice."

Seeing uncertainty in the visitor's face, the man of high rank added in reassurance, "Should you nonetheless think that you detect even the slightest spores of treachery in the air here, let us dispel them for you. We will lead and you may follow at a distance; protocol's guarantee that we do not intend to surround or harm you."

"Good men of New Dawn," replied Chac Ik, convinced now of their hospitable intentions, "I will not unsheathe my longknife. I know that King Smoke Macaw was on his way here with Lady Rainbow, to return her to her father's arms and to request his marital blessing. It is my belief, too, that King Parrotfish has granted this request, thus becoming an unwavering ally of Quetzal Serpent."

Chapter 23

To Capture a Rainbow

War canoes were approaching Eastern Rock at speed. The figure seated at the front of the lead canoe smiled inwardly: there was only a sliver of moon above and the ten canoes and their occupants were painted black, the approaching danger thus as good as invisible to the unsuspecting eye. Too, Bone Drum had armed the war party from Black Stone with a knowledge of the island's geography and the islanders' habits.

Queen Death Bat stood and turned to face the paddlers of her canoe. She allowed her body to rise and fall in time with the canoe's pitching, alternately bending her knees and straightening her legs to maintain her balance. Too, she had to shift her weight from side to side as the canoe listed when currents converged, its narrow design better suited to the more linear currents of White Water. Cupping her hands around her mouth to project her voice, she addressed her warriors. "Success awaits us. The wind blowing over us from

Eastern Rock will betray neither the sound of your paddling nor your Queen's commands. Our bodies are as dark as the water here, but our target guides us to it with its light. We know the location of the sleeping islanders, and they are not many in number. We must first silently ascend the watchtower, to do what the islanders cannot conceive of ever happening and snatch a rainbow from under the gaze of the night sky. Bone Drum's contingent, emerging from the other side of the promontory, will be ready to hem in any islanders who might have chanced upon our presence and rushed to the Princess's aid. Where the stone platform meets the log steps will become the dais of the Princess's second public humiliation, if need be: once they see our prisoner, she of the many colours," scoffed the warrior Queen, "bound and stooping before us, her so-called 'protectors' will hardly dare to oppose us. Nonetheless, lest they, like a snake shedding its skin, discard the wisdom of non-attack, we will have ready an unassailable defence, in retreat using Lady Rainbow as a living shield."

Queen Death Bat turned to face the prow again and spoke now to the wind. "Yes, so unprepared are our 'hosts', so futile for them would be any prolonged combat, especially with their Princess at the mercy of my blade, that they will almost certainly surrender before they truly begin to fight. More to my taste than their immediate resignation, however, would be some token resistance. May I leave Eastern Rock with a second sweet memory: their island's soil stained with blood, even if no more than that shed after the slaughter of a domestic turkey."

The canoes would soon be at the island. Queen Death Bat sat down and paddled, leading her men, her long torso and arms lending a powerful, graceful arc to her strokes. The flotilla separated into two groups. One drifted towards the island's end; the second paddled towards the far side of the promontory. Close now to the light coming from the island, Queen Death Bat and her group hid their faces and torsos by pressing their bodies down inside the canoes' hulls. Only the rear paddler of each canoe remained half erect to steer it to shore. The landing area was limited: a natural crescent in the headland, its form perfected by additional rocks laid out by human hands. Its design was so pronounced that Queen Death Bat, the first to rise, instantly recognised the symbol for and name of the moon goddess, U. She then recalled the story of how the first moon had dared to proudly shine as brightly as the sun. In punishment for her vanity and boldness, the gods had hurled a gigantic hare into her face, the ensuing flow of blood darkening some of her shine. Indeed, the already shrunken moon here seemed to become shyer, suddenly hiding completely behind dark clouds.

"Does this fading moon presage the disappearance of Lady Rainbow… or is it a warning to me that history will write of the failed siege of Eastern Rock?" feared Queen Death Bat. She had experienced a similar foreboding at Quetzal Serpent, when approaching as a sacrilegious thief the Sacred Jaguar and its Heart. She rattle-shook her head in self-control and pulled her hands through her hair to dispel such thoughts, her nervousness tangible in drops of perspiration on her scalp.

Once more the strategist, the warrior Queen took in the details of her surroundings. The small beach led to a steep slope of rocks against which she and her men could hide. Once in the shallows, the men slid carefully over the gunwales one at a time, their Queen watching them; they knew that should any excessive sound be made, the offender's head might well be used to decorate the prow of her canoe on the return journey. Crouching, the men placed the canoes against the crescent of rocks. Leading over the centre of the slope were steps of long, fixed logs, which they ascended. The logs terminated at the edge of a stone platform, below which Queen Death Bat positioned herself. She alone was allowed to peer over the platform. She saw the windowed, four-storeyed tower that Bone Drum had spoken of. Torches illuminated the walls and a brazier crowned the top level. Queen Death Bat and her men waited but could see no signs of guards. She whispered, half to herself, half to the men beside her.

"So far, Bone Drum has foretold the future correctly. It is late, and it seems that the already complacent guards in this remote haven have willingly dulled further the remains of their senses. Forgetfulness of one's duty, however, is a slight to one's ruler and city state. This night, I will administer fitting punishment, carrying far away she who was left in their care, and leaving welts of shame upon the people of Eastern Rock as they reflect on what vigilance might have prevented."

Lighter in movement now that their shields rested on the logs, a designated group of warriors readied their weapons and crept quickly towards the tower. Once there, they flattened their bodies against three of the four square walls, to better merge with the building. Queen Death Bat remained a discreet short distance from the front wall, her gaze fixed on the top stone window. She frowned, for there was unexpected activity there. A head and torso leaned out from the tower, and appeared to look across the area of approach and towards the sea. The head moved slowly from side to side, as if scanning the watery horizon. Apparently satisfied with its visual patrol, the figure withdrew again.

"We will remain immobile for a short while," whispered Queen Death Bat to her men, "should the guardian of the tower return for a second inspec… tion."

The last syllable was barely to be heard, falling vaguely from her lips, for simultaneously Queen Death Bat's blood became as cold as a reptile's at dawn. The silence ended as something inside the tower's base created a rumble that vibrated throughout the whole structure. The guardian reappeared, and this time looked downwards, but could not see the base of the tower due to the projecting stone skirting separating each level. The guardian then studied the area where the platform met the log steps. Curiosity and arrogance colluded to overpower Queen Death Bat's sense of caution, and she stepped out fully from the wall. The guardian did not notice her at first, but she could see that the face had something unnatural about it. The disparate details soon merged to form the features of Chac, the rain god. The eyes of Guardian Chac now challenged the Queen's. A softer visage then appeared next to the former's. This human face – not for the first time – caused Queen Death Bat to halt halfway between movements.

"Lady Rainbow," she hissed loudly, remembering to moderate the volume of her voice, "come to me, your first and only lover, as recorded by the Death Bat tattoos on your body."

Lady Rainbow did not answer, but made clear her disdain for her rapist, raising her head exaggeratedly high and turning away. Guardian Chac positioned himself in front of her, then blew into a large seashell, sounding the alarm.

Queen Death Bat shouted freely. "We will see if Lady Rainbow's protector is an effigy of Chac come to life, or if he spills human blood. Should it be the former, I know that I may die for attempting to strike a god."

Tightening her grip on her spear, she ran the short distance towards the tower, leapt, and at the last moment released her weapon. Guardian Chac did not try to duck or step away, its view of the missile blocked by its own arm and the seashell it held. The sound of the spear tip penetrating leather and flesh was clearly audible to Lady Rainbow, and she gasped. She reached out to catch the already collapsing body, but both of them were next to the low wall; the guardian had involuntarily leaned forward and in his momentum could not be held. He slipped out of her half-grip and fell from the tower. Lady Rainbow watched, a mixture of terrified helplessness and deep sadness suffusing her whole being. The ground seemed to shoot up to meet him. As his body met the stony ground, the weight and angle of the fall snapped the spear he had unwillingly worn. Queen Death Bat called to the remaining warriors waiting at the log steps.

Lady Rainbow saw a line of darkened limbs scuttle towards the tower. "Oversized, two-legged cockroaches are approaching," she said in disgust.

A groan came from the figure lying on the ground.

Queen Death Bat knelt to inspect this puzzling being; Chac-like, yet vulnerable. Then she noticed the protective padding. "A second, harder skin has saved its now clearly mortal wearer from a lethal impact," she concluded. She also understood now the unchanging expression of the face: the eyes were merely painted on the helmet, which was cracked down the forehead. The hooked nose had broken off and lay a few paces away. As blood seeped from under the god mask, Queen Death Bat was reminded that she too was mortal, and shuddered.

As one of her men leaned forward and offered her a knife to deliver the killing cut, the guardian raised his arm in self-defence.

"No," declared the Queen. "'Chac' wishes to live a little longer, and a request from one combatant to another should be given due thought. I will respect this wish. In the role of warrior, I only kill during the fever and the exchanged blows of battle. The fallen dying I leave for the vulture god Kuch, or to sink into their final sleep."

Having been faithful to her battle code of honouring the vanquished, she returned her attention to the tower. She made to enter it at the foot, but was forced to stop. There had to be steps leading up, she thought, but if so they were obscured by the small, unworked pieces of limestone that she saw in front of her. She guessed that the people of Eastern Rock had spread these rocks up the steep spiral of the tower steps, sealing the narrow stairwell and hindering an invader's ascent. A large number of rocks had presumably just shifted and resettled, the outflow now lying strewn at her feet. "So, this was the source of the ill-timed noise that led to our discovery," she thought aloud. "Too, this Chac seemed to be expecting night-time visitors. But if so, how did he and Eastern Rock know of our coming?"

She didn't notice that the Chac figure had turned his head and was watching her with a pained yet satisfied smile.

Queen Death Bat addressed her men directly. "Lady Rainbow is out of our reach. Time does not permit us to remove the rubble or to try to ascend the tower over this rockslide; nor can we risk damaging my precious cargo-to-be in an attempt to smoke her out with fire. Only if we subdue the islanders – who will now be alert – can she still become our trophy as planned, to replace the head of Jaguar Phallus that was played away from us."

Agitated voices from among Queen Death Bat's group unofficially announced Bone Drum's appearance at the tower, accompanied by only a few of the warriors designated him. Immediately, he began his report. "Queen Death Bat, no sooner had we landed than death-bringing points rained down upon us. Many of my contingent will not be returning to their canoes."

"Your impatience made you careless, Bone Drum," she reprimanded him. "The men here waited for my command before leaving their positions. You had strict instructions to wait for our shell-trumpet signal. Mistaking the enemy's alarm for that, you led your group into an ambush. Lady Rainbow is at the top of the tower, and even the grasping arms of the Death Bat are not long enough to reach up and seize her." She paused, observing how Bone Drum smarted at the rebuke. "Too, we are starting to fall behind the racing night. Thus, I wonder: with what redeeming strategy can you surprise me, my distinguished ally?" she asked with unsmiling semi-sarcasm as she leaned her tall form into him, as if ready to wrench an answer from him.

This close, Bone Drum could feel the impatience of her snorting breath upon him, and her men were walling him in. In essence he was alone, for his own New Dawn contingent who had 'escorted' Lady Rainbow to Black Stone were now under house arrest, to ensure his loyalty during this mission and extinguish any possibility of treachery.

Warily, he answered, "Let us build a living ladder of bodies, so that we can still capture Lady Rainbow and leave before the islanders have organised themselves for battle. Enclosing the settlement there is erected a high stockade of logs. The area around the stockade is dangerous to both invaders and defenders; any traverse of the flanks of sharp, unstable lumps of coral requires time and care."

Queen Death Bat's posture became less threatening as she straightened herself again. *Bone Drum, like many high-ranking warriors*, she thought, *remains roughly cut, an unworked stone from deep in the rocks; nevertheless, he is of greater value in this, his natural, raw state, his martial intelligence and his strength unsoftened by a life of ease at court.*

Before she could give the order to erect a human scaffolding, one of her men shouted, "My Queen, our canoes are drifting away."

Queen Death Bat called to the top of the tower, and Lady Rainbow reappeared.

"We must leave you now, up in your watchtower; your makeshift, impoverished palace on this lonely island." Then her tone softened in farewell. "But sooner or later, my arms will ensnare you."

Bone Drum and Queen Death Bat were the first to reach the edge of the stone platform overlooking the crescent-shaped beach. Peering out to sea, they could make out thin objects moving randomly over the dark water. The wind had calmed and they thought they could hear the occasional human voice coming from the sea.

"It seems that the islanders are more than ready," commented Queen Death Bat grimly. "Our canoes have been set adrift. Let us hope that yours, Bone Drum, have not."

Bone Drum led the way to the other side of the promontory, and indeed his canoes were waiting, undisturbed, on the rocks. The party clambered down to them, stumbling, for this area was beyond the reach of any human-made light.

"We dare not overload these remaining canoes. Therefore, your Queen demands that some of you this night make the ultimate sacrifice." Queen Death Bat stared hard at the faces around her, pre-emptively silencing any voice of protest or appeal. "Bone Drum, our best paddlers and I will board first," she commanded, pointing to the fortunate selected ones.

When the canoes were almost full, the remaining warriors began jostling to secure one of the last places. Those abandoned to the island would have very limited options: either fight an overwhelming number of opponents on their own territory and be killed, or look desperately for any unattended canoes with which to follow their party. *My warrior's reputation and my knowledge of this area have guaranteed me a seat in one of the remaining canoes*, thought Bone Drum smugly. *These men are not swimmers, and in any case, the mainland coast is far. A few of them will no doubt try in their desperation to swim away – a doomed attempt, their spirits soon after discovering what dwells at the bottom of the sea.* This image he found darkly amusing, for, though now an ally of Black Stone, he felt little affinity with his new comrades.

Men of Eastern Rock appeared at the edge of the platform, carrying torches and weapons. They looked down at the area between themselves and Black Stone's retreating canoes and saw, standing on the water-swept rocks, their victims-to-be, neither truly on land nor at sea, unable to advance or retreat. The glare of many torches, flaming brightly in the strong breeze, half-blinded the eyes that beheld them from below. Thus, most of the trapped warriors of Black Stone could not see until the last moment an approaching volley of spears. Fearing a second volley, some of the survivors jumped into the water in the vain hope of escape, but their heads soon disappeared, not to resurface. Watching from his canoe, Bone Drum nodded to himself at the accuracy of his prediction.

The canoes had already travelled a few dozen strokes, and were now passing a cluster of half-submerged boulders. They would soon be out of the reach of pursuing spears. "How can those warriors on land hope to catch us here," jeered one of Queen Death Bat's men as he looked back towards the rocks, "we who now race away safely across the Great Blue Water?"

His question was swiftly answered. Objects flew out of the water and over the canoes, dropping on the opposite sides. There was a thudding sound as skeletal claws clamped down upon the gunwales, holding something web-like firmly in place. Screams born of a terror of the supernatural came from the canoes, as the occupants felt the powerful web pressing into their skin. They struggled to stand up, only partly succeeding in pushing against their flexible cage. In response the web tightened yet more, trapping the heads and necks of those still seated. The canoes listed violently.

"A local deity is punishing Black Stone's trespass of Eastern Rock and threat to Lady Rainbow," said one paddler.

"These webs must have been spun by a giant spider god of the sea," said another.

"These are no webs," yelled Bone Drum from the prow of his canoe, "they are fishing nets, and the claws you see are grappling hooks. We are under attack from islanders swimming beneath us." Indeed, now and then a human hand rested – for the briefest of moments – on the gunwales. "Cut the net with your knives," urged Bone Drum.

Those who could wriggle free of the interlocking constraints of squatting-block and net drew their knives, but for many, Bone Drum's words came too late, for some of the canoes capsized, their paddlers still held fast like insects in a true spider's web. Bone Drum peered into the darkness, hoping to locate the Queen's canoe; though he was the guide here, Queen Death Bat was the true commander of this mission, and only her continued presence and commands might inspire their men to recreate order from this chaos. He saw human bodies swimming away from the scene; obviously the ambushers returning to their comrades at the rocks. Then he recognised a voice, its imperious resonance clear even above the noise of thrashing, drowning men.

"Bone Drum, your Queen is over here. Come to her aid."

He dived into the water and swam the short distance to the source of the command. He found Queen Death Bat barely treading water whilst trying to pull herself back to her estranged canoe via a length of net still anchored to a gunwale. He steered towards her a floating corpse, and she hauled herself onto it. Using the corpse's neck as a hold, Bone Drum swam, pulling the corpse and Queen Death Bat through the water.

"A curious water-craft for a Queen," she panted to herself, "yet fitting for I, whose totem is Zotz, the Bat of Death."

It was living hands that reached down from a canoe to lift her and her rescuer out of the water. They were immediately given weapons, and they understood why: approaching was a foreign flotilla. Queen Death Bat quickly forgot her near-drowning: the emblem at the prow of the oncoming lead canoe displayed the oversized, outspread wings of a bird, and accompanying flashes of red and yellow permeated the darkness.

"Smoke Macaw," she said, pulling her dripping hair away from her eyes and applying a clasp to it. She extended her open forearms, preparing to offer fond welcome, an expression of contentment and sensuality upon her face.

Her inappropriate intimacy startled and angered Bone Drum. "This man is our enemy and we have just tried to kidnap his beloved," he reminded her.

"Bone Drum," she replied, "we have lost many canoes, their paddlers lifeless and of no more use to us than driftwood. Smoke Macaw and I have fought before, albeit without weapons, at the ball court near Water in Stone. We can put down our weapons. He is not a ruler who, in the thoughtlessness of rage, would cut down opponents unwilling to engage in battle."

"Queen Death Bat," advised Bone Drum, "whatever his goal, to me it is clear that he expects some of our blood to colour the water here. Look."

She watched the canoes more closely, and indeed their occupants' movements did not seem conciliatory: spears were being drawn back in the launching position, and the speed of the canoes was increasing.

"We still have a chance to paddle out of the range of attack," said Bone Drum.

"You are right," agreed Queen Death Bat. "Perhaps I have counted too much on Smoke Macaw's mildness." *Perhaps, too*, she thought, *on his attraction to me.*

She gave the command to paddle at double speed, but in their haste, the two lead canoes collided, blocking and rerouting the paths of the others. This small loss of time allowed the pursuers to gain distance upon the pursued, keeping the Black Stone flotilla, as Smoke Macaw told his men, "within reach of retribution's fist".

Queen Death Bat cursed as she looked behind her: glowing, trailing objects were in the air. They reached the rearmost of her fleeing canoes, either landing with a hiss in the water or finding a random target among the compact line of bodies. She stood up. Moving nimbly along the canoe, she threw two of those already dead overboard. Amidst the howling of those struck by flaming spears, she yelled, "Warriors of Black Stone, get rid of any limp ballast, and paddle faster if you do not wish to finish your life cooked on a spit like a collared peccary." Then she realised the import of her own words: while standing, she was easy to see and single out as a target. Indeed, she now became aware of something approaching her at eye level. She jerked her head to one side – too late to avoid a sharp caress, accompanied by a passing blowing sound. Clapping her hand to the side of her face, she detected softness and warmth. On examining her hand, red liquid confirmed what she had suspected, though only half-felt: there was a gash under her eye and her earlobe had been torn. Reminded of her unusually large, prominent ears, she thought, *Perhaps it is a local god's grim joke: an attempt to pierce my ear and adorn it with a pointed bolt; near-death's earring. I hereby make a willing offering of my spilt blood to the gods of war, as an advance tribute in return for their allowing me, the warrior Queen, to live and continue her ambitions of conquest and empire.*

The attacking flotilla spread out, hemming in Queen Death Bat's. King Smoke Macaw's canoe had separated from its vanguard, to travel unseen in the darkness. Now it emerged from that darkness and, with a last spurt of paddling, rammed Queen Death Bat's. From behind a prow-wall of shields, Smoke Macaw emerged, grimacing like a wrathful deity. He leapt onto the enemy vessel, snarling, "Too long have I suppressed my anger at the murder of my father, the sacrilegious theft of the Heart, and Bone Drum's treachery. These crimes have been mere glowing coals, but now will roar a fire of vengeance, enflamed by incessant harassment, kidnapping of rank, and defamatory rape. Let my enemies shrink before my rage."

From the other end of the canoe, Queen Death Bat was watching. Aroused at the thought of the impassioned attack about to be unleashed, she breathed in deeply the fragrance of approaching danger, relishing the prospect of what for her was a combination of combat and mating ritual. *This violent foreplay, a prelude to a future in which Smoke Macaw will be naked beneath me... how wildly races my blood!*

Smoke Macaw held a round shield in one hand, and in the other a globe-headed royal sceptre of white stone, the shaft incised in red with protective glyphs of cinnabar. This short staff of rank could double as a weapon. The shield he used first, to intercept a spear thrown at him from another canoe; he then snapped the audacious missile in two over his leather-armoured thigh, leaving part of it hanging from his shield. Meanwhile, Quetzal Serpent's canoes continued to penetrate Black Stone's disorientated flotilla, the former disgorging more boarders from behind their shields. The enemy warrior nearest to Smoke Macaw swung a paddle at him, using the pointed head as an impromptu blade. Smoke Macaw retreated slightly and the paddle missed its mark.

Unchecked by contact with another object, the attacker's own momentum created a follow-through of the slashing movement, pulling him into his opponent's space. In riposte, Smoke Macaw swung his sceptre-mace towards the man's head. Stone met bone as the weapon impacted the thin cranial skin, a muffled crack announcing the man's immediate death. He fell at Smoke Macaw's feet, and Smoke Macaw stepped onto the corpse as onto a pedestal; a demonstrative symbol of his victory.

A second adversary leapt at Smoke Macaw, hacking at his head with an axe. Smoke Macaw raised his shield to block the blow; already damaged by the spear, it was now eviscerated by the sharpness and force of the descending weapon, a deep hole in its leather surface revealing its innards of layered wood. Smoke Macaw deliberated momentarily as to whether to discard his shield. The attacker, encouraged by his initial success, grinned and raised his axe again. His blow-hand, at that midpoint between rising and falling, hung behind him and put him fractionally off balance. Smoke Macaw lunged low and at an angle, his shield pushing the surprised axeman to the side of the canoe, where he tripped over the gunwale and fell into the sea.

Smoke Macaw sheathed his mace, to temporarily free both hands. A third, spear-wielding opponent was unable to follow his flow of movement as Smoke Macaw swung his shield in a devastating arc that dislodged the spear, then thudded into the side of the man's torso. Large splinters from the shield embedded into his skin, and the man groaned and collapsed, stunned by the blow. Smoke Macaw discarded his shield. Swinging and parrying with his mace, he advanced unrelentingly along the canoe, a line of opponents parting in death before him. Reaching the other end, he raised his mace to strike the final figure still standing. The figure's apparent lack of concern caused him to check himself, there suddenly no longer being an obvious adversary to strike. He shook his head, aware that he had very nearly submitted to uncontrolled fury, and his battle-crazed eyes calmed.

He realised that he was looking at Queen Death Bat. There was a confidence in her face that robbed him of his own, and for the first time since he had boarded the canoe, its narrowness made him feel unsure of his balance. Bracing legs and mind, his centredness – without and within – returned. Now he looked at her with cool neutrality, and neither pleasure nor anger apparent on his face. The fighting in the other canoes had stopped, the occupants awaiting the outcome of their rulers' encounter. Smoke Macaw motioned to his men to transfer to the Queen's canoe two fresh torches and the macaw-feather standard. His tongue remained as inexpressive as his face as he moved in closer to her. He began to remove her heavy necklace of jade skulls. She offered no resistance; indeed, she opened up her neck to him, allowing his fingers unhindered access to her skin.

The King of Quetzal Serpent held up the warrior Queen's necklace. "Behold our battle trophy," he called out.

Queen Death Bat's men dropped their weapons.

"King Smoke Macaw is merciful now, Death Bat. Should, however, Black Stone engage Quetzal Serpent in further conflict, I will, under the gaze of your own subjects, personally strip you not only of your adornments, but also your royal clothing."

Initially, Smoke Macaw's proximity – gained by exemplary ferocity, thought Queen Death Bat – had intoxicated her.

Now, with her flotilla routed and her necklace gone, she scowled long at the threat of this unsurpassed humiliation. Handing the necklace to one of his men, Smoke Macaw gave her a silent command, pointing to the coast and then inland: that area where White Water flowed near Water in Stone and back to Black Stone. She knew that carrying his standard would guarantee her party diplomatic immunity; unmolested passage back to Black Stone. Glancing to either side of her, she saw that his canoes outnumbered and surrounded her own. They had, in fact, separated her canoe and Bone Drum's from the rest of her flotilla.

"So, the Black Stone canoes behind the demarcation line will not be accompanying us," she concluded aloud. She looked into the eyes of the doomed men. Some looked back proudly; others showed fear. She sat down, with a lack of physical grace unusual for her, to begin her bootyless journey back to Black Stone. She noticed movement in the water: cutting through the surface was something wedge-like and sharply angled, atop a smooth grey-black base. The head of a giant fish unfamiliar to her appeared and dragged away a corpse. *The dead from the Middle Realm become food for the living of the Great Blue Water*, she reflected. *Such a creature could have also pulled away my earlier corpse-raft, or even attacked me or Bone Drum.* The prospect both fascinated and terrified her.

She ordered her canoes to halt. Looking back, she and her men saw a large fire. "Death waits impatiently for our warriors there," declared the Queen. "Flames are rushing in to finish the work begun by flying blades and a king's orb of stone. The orb of stone," she repeated. "Just as Smoke Macaw has robbed me of my jade necklace, so will I one day – I vow to the gods – relieve him of his sceptre-mace. So continues the cycle of battle and reprisal, until there is a clear victor. I will return Smoke Macaw's present punishment by fire, and myself burn the life out of Quetzal Serpent. As my captive, the former King will watch as I torture his beloved Green-Eyed Lady Rainbow on his own temple steps. Wishing to stop her pain, he will become my willing slave."

There Queen Death Bat finished giving details, for her future sexual liaisons – albeit through coercion – would be with the King of Quetzal Serpent, and she did not want to create further suspicion or even jealousy in her present ally.

Chapter 24

Chac and the Priest

Queen Death Bat sat on her palace steps. The stone was still cool from the night air. She had been there since long before the sun had begun to extinguish the myriad stars which equalled in number the countless thoughts in her head. Her eyes bored into the black stone in unison with the knife blade she was using to scrape out a tiny heap of dust from the step she sat on. Two frustrating months of twenty days each had passed since her canoe fleet's defeat at Eastern Rock, which had also weakened support from some of her allies.

Too, she thought, *Bone Drum's often casual, even impudent behaviour towards his Queen is irritating. Like a bothersome insect, he will one day have the life squashed out of him.* During those nights when Bone Drum was clumsily atop her, she had wished it was Smoke Macaw sharing his body with her. She felt an emptiness inside her as wide as the sky viewed from the temple peak. On some days, her hunger for Smoke Macaw's affections was so great that she spurned both worldly and psychic nourishment, indifferent to solid maize or liquid *balche*. Bone Drum and his men had only superficially integrated themselves into Black Stone society, participating in weapons practice and patrol duty by day and attending court meals in the evenings; otherwise, they kept company among themselves. The Queen remained aware, however, that the begrudgingly accepted warriors from New Dawn could still be of use in her final assault on Quetzal Serpent.

On a finger, she counted a third undesirable development: as she'd fled Eastern Rock, one of her eyes had been injured. Her priest Nine Stars, also responsible for healing, had so far been unable to much improve its condition, though he had supplied a salve to lessen the pain. She was gradually losing the sight of that eye: *It will soon desert my warrior's head.* This was not the only disappointment she had experienced from him. *Clearly*, she concluded, *Nine Stars' shortcomings have so far outweighed his achievements. Thus, I must think of an exceptional challenge for him, to give him an opportunity – under extremely demanding circumstances – to truly show his dedication to his patron and Queen.*

Nine Stars stood bewildered in the middle of the grassy square before the palace. He could not yet think with full clarity: after spending the night with the subordinate priests, observing and recording the positions of the moon, Venus and various stars, his subsequent rest period had been prematurely ended by an urgent summons to present himself here. As his eyes grew less blurred, he noticed with foreboding that a section of the square had been freshly worked.

A voice from behind jolted him. "Nine Stars, Black Stone's shameful experience at Eastern Rock was due to your imprecise calculations and unwise advice," said Queen Death Bat, speaking from atop a litter borne by four men. "Our city lost some of its best warriors, along with a number of canoes. Our mission was a failure, for we left without our intended prisoner. As a result, Smoke Macaw remains blinded by his supposed love for Green Eyed Lady Rainbow, and thus beyond my influence. What is to become of 'our' great plans, Nine Stars?" she asked, sneeringly referring to the time when she had assured him of his place in her future; when they had together handled and admired the Heart of the Jaguar.

"My Queen, the timing of your attack was prophesied as being perfect," countered Nine Stars. "I stood at one of the three doors of our circular star tower, and there I saw the goddess Lahun Chan in the most favourable position for war in her present 584-K'in cycle."

"Either that star has changed her character and is no longer to be trusted," retorted Queen Death Bat, "or Black Stone's astronomer-priest has a head that is ageing before it is truly old. It is time we had a public display of how well our priest can master the unexpected; of how quickly he can think in a situation of… great personal danger."

Two warriors took Nine Stars' arms and, their undimmed respect for their priest evident in their light grip (though following Queen Death Bat's orders, they were not comfortable with their task), guided him further out into the square, where he was released. He walked to what he was sure was the epicentre of his fate, stopping at the edge of a pit. A crowd gathered around him, reinforcing his sense of the inevitability of today's events.

Queen Death Bat spoke loudly to him and to the others present. "Nine Stars, your actions here in this Xibalba in miniature will determine your future. If you pass this trial, you will be merely banished from Black Stone. Perhaps you will be accepted for the rest of your time in the Middle Realm as a priest elsewhere. If that happens, you and I will meet again somewhere in my empire, for one day all Maya will serve me as their supreme and only ruler." She paused. "If you do not pass today's trial, your fate, depending on my whim, may be that of the captain of a losing team at *pok ta pok*. Buried without the proper rites, you will not join other high priests as a shooting star to be seen and remembered in nights of this and coming cycles."

The priest stared at her, unable to believe that his Queen would treat him as a criminal or prisoner of war, albeit one privileged with the possibility of a royal pardon.

"Let Nine Stars be prepared," said Queen Death Bat.

Two slaves came forward and removed his gown. Their appearance reflected Nine Stars' feeling of relegation: once relatively free maize-gatherers, they now bore the stigmatic, strap-like scar that crossed the mouth and reached from ear to ear, symbolising sacrifice; albeit here in a non-lethal form: that of unbroken servitude. Wondering if he would need bodily protection, Nine Stars realised that he was wearing only a top and a skirt of cotton, and sandals. As if to confirm his presentiment of imminent, intense physical activity, his still-hanging, sight-obstructing hair – driven out of bed, he had had no time to properly make his toilet – was pulled up and back into a topknot and tightened, and he was given a long drink of papaya juice mixed with water. A ladder was placed inside the pit and Queen Death Bat indicated that he should descend. A slave accompanied him. The slant-walled pit was deep twice the height of a man and wide eight arm-lengths. Its intense colour seemed threatening to Nine Stars: the orange-red haematite soil that normally went unseen, yet lay so shallowly beneath the visible layer of trees, plants and grass. In the middle of the levelled floor was a large stone from the river, flat and smooth.

"Give the priest his weapons," the warrior Queen called down from a standing position in her litter.

The slave who had joined him in the pit removed a length of cloth carried on his back and unwrapped its folds, presenting in his outstretched hands the cloth's contents to the priest. Nine Stars inspected the longknife and the pole ending in a double prong, wondering what kind of opponent the latter might be for. The second slave descended and removed from his shoulder a large ceramic pot held in a net. He placed it on the ground next to the stone. Both slaves then returned to the top of the pit and the ladder was withdrawn.

"Nine Stars," called Queen Death Bat again, "I command you to break the pot with the stone."

Nine Stars suddenly felt cold and very alone, despite the multitude of faces watching him from above. He picked up the stone, his hands trembling at the thought of what he was about to unleash. Committing himself, he inhaled deeply and quickly brought down the stone upon the pot. The pot shattered into several pieces and no supernatural wind or fire escaped, but something just as fear-inspiring: a sound reminiscent of a music-rattle. Nine Stars could now guess who his challenger was, and he jumped back. Words filled the pit, echoing from its centre, he thought at first, but when he angled his ear in the direction of the broken pot, he realised that they came from above him: it was his Queen again, her voice barely audible in its terrible whisper.

"Pick up your weapons. Your two companions of the pit were much harassed before being transferred to the pot. They are irritable, and they can be tenacious fighters."

Nine Stars took the forked staff – or bident – in his left hand and the longknife in his right. "I am an astronomer-priest. What would a warrior do to prepare for battle?" he wondered aloud. He jabbed the bident at an imaginary warrior and tested the longknife's weight, slashing it experimentally through the air. He looked back at the shards of the ceramic vessel and felt – strangely, he thought – relief, for the suspense was over. His opponent had entered the arena, its form as he had predicted: dark orbs as eyes; the body long and trailing, as thick as a man's arm. Was it one of the manifestations of Chac, the rain god, whose visage of gaping mouth and stylised, curling nose adorned the facades of buildings in the plain region, where he was especially revered?

The snake, a fer-de-lance, raised its head, opening its mouth to reveal two curved white fangs. Its tail shook and sounded; the colour and form of the rattle resembled kernels of maize, whose growth was triggered by the seasonal rains heralded by the appearance of rattlesnakes in the fields. Feeling threatened when the much larger opponent before it did not retreat, the snake lunged at Nine Stars, its fangs now truly become a living weapon. The strike missed, and the snake re-coiled its body.

Nine Stars now felt indignation, not fear. *It is unheard of for a high priest to be put to trial by combat. There have not even been the obligatory judicial proceedings, nor an official recording of the verdict by a scribe.* His anger gave him new strength: as the snake lunged at him a second time, he parried the attack with the bident, knocking the snake to the ground.

"Wave the longknife at ground level, at the snake's head," advised Queen Death Bat. "When it bites at the tip of the blade, bring the fork from behind the snake's head and pin it to the ground, then strike with the knife."

The priest was grateful for these words of instruction; from she who was the paragon of agility both as a ball player and as a warrior. The snake indeed faltered before the longknife, but then retreated. Nine Stars followed it, goading with the knife as the snake slithered back towards the net and the pot shards. The priest had foreseen this and reached the snake's sought-for sanctuary before it, pinning its neck to the ground with the bident. Unpractised in the use of such a large blade, he instead used the flat side of the longknife, bringing it down upon the snake's head several times in succession. The snake stopped moving, and Nine Stars relaxed, inwardly congratulating himself.

Victory's sweet draught soon turned bitter when a second fer-de-lance emerged slowly from the shadows of the net and the pot shards. To Nine Stars' surprise, this one did not lunge, but opened its mouth and sprayed something at him. Remembering that the Fluid of Death flowed through the bodies of such snakes, he realised that it was venom that had just spattered his cheek and shoulder. *I have perhaps escaped blindness by as little space as a knife's edge*, he thought. More comfortable now with his weapons, and feeling familiar with the behaviour of a 'companion of the pit', he immediately began to close the distance between the snake and himself. *As I hoped, my swaying longknife is again confusing my opponent. I will use this advantage to help me defeat this demon released from a ceramic cage*, he decided. His prediction became truth. He managed to immobilise the snake with the fork, and with the longknife cut into its neck three times, separating its head from its body.

The priest turned and took a few steps, the better to look up at his Queen. He was sure of her approval of his performance.

Instead, she gave him yet more advice. "Nine Stars, is it wise to turn your back on an enemy the moment they have fallen?"

He brought his gaze back to the floor of the pit. He could not trust his eyes: the undulating body was moving in one direction and the severed head in another – towards him, its mouth wide open. Suddenly understanding his opponent's true identity, Nine Stars dropped his weapons and knelt on the ground, his own bowed head looking submissively at the head approaching him. "Terror of the forest, bringer of the rains, forgive my arrogance. I did not recognise you for who you truly are. But now I see you, Lord Chac, risen again from the butchered flesh before me, reborn. In penance, I offer up my life…"

He stopped speaking, nearly gasping at the snake's repeated stabs into his thigh. He watched his punisher, somehow managing not to jerk in reaction to the pain. A spear lodged itself in the ground near the snake's head. The ladder was lowered into the pit, but Queen Death Bat was quicker: she leapt in, absorbing the impact of contact with the pit floor by bending her knees, and in one continuous movement rolled forward and to the side. Retrieving her spear, she stabbed the snake's head and disengaged it from the priest's leg. Impaled on the spear, the head quivered briefly, and then was still.

Nine Stars started to sway. Though he was losing consciousness, his vision fading, he could see that his Queen was staring at him: he was bleeding from the nose; his body's reaction to the multiple snakebites. Finally, he collapsed to the ground and was carried out of the pit on a litter, but Queen Death Bat remained, to reflect on the outcome of this 'unique encounter', as she termed it.

"In my disappointment with the accuracy of his oracles, I have been hasty in seeking to lash humility into my overambitious priest," she murmured in realisation. "Have I, in humiliating and wounding him, done myself a disservice of monumental proportions, inadvertently dislodging the cornerstone of Black Stone; namely its subjects' unshakeable belief in their city's divinely ordained supremacy?" She looked at the bodies of the snakes, then at the priest's abandoned weapons. "I was sure Nine Stars would prove his skill and his commitment to his Queen today – and he did, until the crucial moment. I was negligent in my preparation of the snakes, and must do penance, for I failed to determine whether either of the snakes captured for this contest," here she glanced at the shattered ceramic pot, "was of the variety that, unlike a sacrificed human, continues to fight even after decapitation; a sight to terrorise the most courageous of warriors. I myself have just killed such a snake. Nine Stars spoke earlier of the divinity of his opponent. Not for the first time, I hope I have not misinterpreted what I see, for, if he was right, I may endure an afterlife worse than my priest's present suffering. For the verdict Chac chooses to hand down, even to a Queen, may be thus: the blasphemer is condemned to hear his own heart booming in unbearable fear as he is pursued along subterranean tunnels for eternity; a giant, vengeful Chac just far enough behind to give the pursued the hope of not being run down and impaled on double fangs."

Queen Death Bat ascended the ladder. Facing her subjects once more, she saw the uncertainty in their eyes that mirrored her own deep concern over the empty space created in their hierarchy.

Black Stone no longer has a high priest to communicate with the gods, said a voice within her.

There are acolytes – the Queen met the accusing eyes of her alter ego – *one of whom can assume the title of high priest until Jungle Tortoise serves Black Stone.*

Yes, but only Nine Stars has the authority to select an appropriate interim successor, came the irrefutable reply.

Then his earlier statement about the interdependence of ruler and high priest has proved correct, Queen Death Bat was forced to accede.

Her address to her subjects, however, would differ greatly in tone. As she emerged from the pit, the dense crowd around its rim opened up. They followed her as she proceeded to the miniature, flat-topped pyramid that lay halfway between her palace and the main temple. She ascended the few steps of the pyramid, which was essentially a low platform for quickly communicating news and official statements.

"Jungle Tortoise of Quetzal Serpent will be our new priest," she declared, "and there can be none better than he who is also a shaman-astronomer. Yes – when Quetzal Serpent has become our captive of war, Jungle Tortoise will serve a new ruler. He will not risk incurring the wrath of the

Death Bat, who would answer a refusal to serve us with a mass sacrifice of Quetzal Serpent's people."

She saw a flicker of hope light up in her subjects' eyes. She motioned to her most esteemed warriors, and they ascended the platform to stand alongside her. Bone Drum was not among them; the memory of his role in the unsuccessful attempt to kidnap Lady Rainbow might now lessen her subjects' renewing confidence.

"I bid you speak," said the warrior Queen to her commander.

"I have organised our provisions, and our fresh weapons hungrily await the taste of Quetzal Serpent's blood. Give us the word and we will notify our allies that we are ready to lead them to victory on the high plateau."

Queen Death Bat had wanted more time to formulate a campaign strategy, but her own actions had accelerated her city state's re-entry into armed conflict with Quetzal Serpent. The events at Eastern Rock had greatly weakened Black Stone's morale, and the latter's subjects urgently needed a reaffirming display of leadership. If she did not act soon, Black Stone's allies too might lose their enthusiasm for participating in what was, for them, becoming a foreign feud. "Warriors and subjects of Black Stone," she announced, "in this month, the star-planet Lahun Chan, now harbinger of war, will write in blood the final chapter in the annals of Quetzal Serpent, then slam shut the book, dust quickly settling upon it. Newly commissioned monuments and murals at the city on the high plateau will never be finished, the existing ones defiled by us. We will gouge out glyphs, crack open stelae and smear murals. With its people vanquished, its buildings demolished and its visual history erased, Quetzal Serpent's defeat will be total."

Her subjects cheered, overjoyed at their ruler's pledges of final dominance over their prestigious rival. Upon leaving the platform, the warriors flanked their Queen and were themselves mobbed, so great was the crowd's excitement at Queen Death Bat's description of Black Stone's glory to come.

Chapter 25

The Merging of Macaw and Orchid

A small contingent of guards remained at Open Sky Cenote with Smoke Macaw and Lady Rainbow. The other warriors, again led by Jungle Tortoise, had continued on to Quetzal Serpent, above the twisting, riverine forest and the unannounced, precipitous canyons. Despite the discreet use of a few torches, the overnight portion of this march over uneven ground would be slower than the outbound one. The lighting-beetles were no longer to be found; their presence was tied to high humidity, and the weather was becoming drier.

The death of Chac Ik, Rain God on the Wind, who had become a comforter and a friend to Lady Rainbow as she waited with a mixture of longing and fear for the arrivals of both her love and her foe; Smoke Macaw's exposure to danger as he had led the battle at sea; and finally his long return journey, not yet finished. These events had the cumulative effect of a strong sleeping draught on Lady Rainbow from the moment she and the war party reached the lagoon. Smoke Macaw carried her to his canoe, laying blankets and robes under and around her for warmth and comfort. Before joining his men for a meal, he remained at the canoe awhile. It was a clear night, almost a full moon, and he gazed long upon his beloved's face, her breathing loud and her mouth half-open in the deep relief that overdue rest brings. In her makeshift bed, she moved many times and murmured incomprehensibly, but Smoke Macaw did not mind that he could not understand her. He wanted to bring her back from her dream with kisses, but instead let her sleep unbroken.

Later he returned from dining, bringing with him a bowl of crayfish stew and a gourd of water, should Lady Rainbow awake and need refreshments. Approaching their shelter for the night, he appraised its form and supporting structures. The canoe was flanked on either side by another canoe, bound to the central vessel by double cross-poles, thus lending stability. The construction as a whole resembled, thought Smoke Macaw, the insects – aptly named water boatmen – that by day skittered over the water's surface. The sturdy craft could not, however, completely defy the air and water around it: in the ensuing strong breeze, its minimal rocking lulled to sleep the weary but contented Smoke Macaw as he lay, wrapped in a blanket, at Lady Rainbow's feet.

I hope that I may enter Lady Rainbow's dream world this night, he thought as his eyes closed.

Smoke Macaw's desire for Lady Rainbow had woken him early. He positioned himself in the middle canoe of the three, the better to steer the multiple-outrigger. He long-poled to a shaded part of the lagoon, under the boughs of a tree whose branches hung down and nearly touched the water, the area around it obscured by reeds and a large boulder. Facing the gunwale, he squatted and let sink a heavy anchor-stone, paying out the line slowly, then tugged briefly to check the stone's fastness. Satisfied, he stood up.

When something pushed him from behind, he did not resist, but let his body flow with the force of the impact, going overboard in a diving posture. He heard a voice, muffled by the sound of his entering the water. Knife in hand, he resurfaced. Expecting danger, he was confronted instead by laughter – wonderfully pleasant to hear – and saw why: Lady Rainbow was awake. Her foot was braced against the gunwale, and she was looking deeply into his eyes.

"Smoke Macaw, what would your subjects say if they had seen how easily an enemy might creep up on their King?" she teased.

Leisurely, Smoke Macaw got back into the canoe.

"So, my love," she continued, "it seems my 'attack' means as little to you as the water now dripping from your body."

In answer, he gently put his arms around her, from behind. He laid his head against hers and gently swayed their bodies from side to side. Suddenly, he leaned outwards from the canoe. Lady Rainbow shrieked in surprise as they started to fall. Still holding her, he turned in mid-air, so that their faces would not hit the water with the combined weight of their bodies. Nonetheless, he spluttered as water entered his mouth.

Lady Rainbow took a quick, deep breath and submerged before Smoke Macaw had time to turn his head and locate her. *Smoke Macaw*, she thought, *perhaps you have forgotten the murals at New Dawn; that I am almost as at ease in water as on land. Let me playfully remind you of this.* She was now beneath him, and could see that he was rotating at the water's surface, trying to locate her. She turned as he did, remaining at depth and behind him. When he finally stopped turning, she ascended, her arms outstretched in front of her. She exhaled half of her air to become less buoyant, grabbed his ankles, and jerked downwards. She reassured herself of his swift reaction to the immersion; that this unexpected game would not injure him. *Did not he too learn to master, even to revel in, time spent underwater – in this very cenote – when a child? Has he not recounted to me how he held his breath when diving at Water in Stone to search for the Heart of the Jaguar? Yes, and I have seen for myself his courage in unknown waters, when we swam together with the shark deities in the sea of my birth.*

She could have prolonged their play – her pre-dive hyperventilation would allow her a little additional time below the surface – but she felt a longing inside her, and it was not for air. She released her human 'catch' and swam upwards. Simultaneously, Smoke Macaw's head burst through the surface next to her, and he turned in her direction and smiled. He gave her his hand and they swam together to the canoe. Holding the gunwale with one hand, with his other he held her to him and kissed her several times, each time longer than the last. She found she was hyperventilating again, this time from pleasure. Wondering if her spinning head might cause her to lose consciousness and, despite his half-embrace, slip downwards and away from him, she placed both arms on his shoulders. Now she tilted her head slightly downwards, her green eyes shining and piercing his. Smoke Macaw understood. To help her into the canoe, he pushed up against her bottom, but could not resist the temptation to pinch it at the same time. She looked back at him in mock indignation, and then gave him a girlish smile.

They stood in the canoe, facing each other. He found her wet, uncombed hair beautiful. His hands trembled a little as he removed her wrap. The water from her hair was running over her breasts; he lowered his head to trail his tongue over the curved, smooth skin, then lingered at her nipples, sucking now gently, now firmly. She nuzzled his head between her breasts, then pulled it up again to meet her lips. They walked hand in hand to the prow of the canoe, where they dried each other's torsos with long cloths. She knelt down upon her wrap and dragged her tongue up the muscles of his stomach, probing his navel. Pressing her cheek against his loincloth, she could feel his hardness. In her inexperience, she was unable to properly untie the loincloth and so yanked it downwards and off, causing him to yell, and her to half-laugh.

Her expression became serious again as she pulled him slowly down on top of her. They were again where they had awoken, among the blankets and cloaks. She supported his weight with her arms, her palms just below his pectorals and her fingertips brushing his nipples. In each other's eyes they saw that unique ray of light, reflected back and forth between them. Her lower lips felt warm, as if dusted with a very mild chilli pepper.

"Smoke Macaw, my love," she said, "let the water-drenched coolness of your manhood soothe the spice of my ardour." She watched, for the first time and with fascination, that part of him that was to transform her. "My damp cave awaits the entry of the one-eyed serpent." Then she welcomed him into that mysterious place, held in awe since the appearance of the first Maya.

She allowed him to enter further. When she felt his tension turning into mild aggression, she pressed him fully to her. He let out a long, deep moan. Slowly she guided him away from her, her hands pushing against his chest, then relaxed in increments her support, causing him to enter her once more. She repeated the movements several times. At one now with the rhythm of man and woman, it was he who regulated their lovemaking. She writhed under him, her head flailing against the softness of the blankets, as she twice experienced the measured pleasure of the foothills of ecstasy, before descending again to the valley of contentment. Now she was ready to ascend with him to the peak of the mountain.

"Share with me your essence," she whispered.

Smoke Macaw was a demigod, yes, but he was also a man, and the sound of her words disturbed his concentration, leaving him feeling helpless. She reassured him, stroking back his hair that had worked loose from its topknot, and smiling at him. Once again, she guided him into her; he soon regained his rhythm, watching and revelling in the way her hips shook ever so slightly as he stabbed her in love. His voice thundered as the volcano inside him erupted, his pent-up magma finally released. Lady Rainbow sighed violently and arched her back to receive fully the sacred liquid; she knew that it would set to form a lava tunnel, moulded by her own tunnel of inner flesh, and that from this would emerge, nine lunar cycles later, the head of their child. She could see his eyes glistening with a deep sense of relief.

He did not withdraw, however, but only raised his hips a little, remaining partially joined to her. He looked into her eyes; through them; down, down inside her and beyond; then let his body fall gently onto hers, and she held his head close to hers and pulled a blanket over them. Lying silently together in rest, they could feel the floating framework shifting subtly on the water, the wake of their lovemaking massaging their spirits yet further. She felt him become active again, and removed the blanket. Gently, he dropped multiple kisses on her lips, then her breasts. Moving further down her body, he glided his cheek across the curve of her belly. Now his lips and tongue were drawn irresistibly to the centre of her, into which he had just poured from his innermost self. She held his head firmly against her; for Smoke Macaw it was her altar, and she moaned as he worshipped her.

Chapter 26

Embracing Ixtab

Queen Death Bat had issued her challenge to Quetzal Serpent. She had also informed the settlements and minor cities of the unprecedented event to come: instead of waging a possibly drawn-out and complicated war – her present allies might, without warning, defect to Quetzal Serpent – her chosen warrior would fight to the death Smoke Macaw's. The vanquished opponent's ruler would then be obliged to cede their city temple and territory to the victor.

Smoke Macaw's sense of responsibility towards all his subjects, and his pride in his reputation, meant that he could not allow the avoidable death in his name of one of his warriors. He also knew that he could not simply ignore or refuse a request to combat – in such a case, the only non-military solution acceptable to Queen Death Bat would be Quetzal Serpent's unconditional surrender. As at the ball game, Smoke Macaw unexpectedly compromised the

Queen's plans. "I will wield myself the weapons that clash with those of the challenger," was the reply delivered to her.

To this self-endangerment on the King's part the warrior Queen reluctantly agreed; their cities lay two days' travel apart and she wished to avoid further delays caused by negotiations conducted over that distance.

Lady Rainbow reacted to Smoke Macaw's determination to represent himself in battle thus: "My love, Queen Death Bat's nameless defender will surely be Bone Drum. Knowing that I am yours, and willingly so, he may well discover within him an almost inhuman strength. The scene of your and Bone Drum's battle waits to be recorded in stone – circumstances demand nothing less – but know that my participation too is irrevocable; that the stonemasons must also chisel my form into the scene. I will fight alongside you against Bone Drum. I know that he will, at least, not wish to harm me, and this should weaken his warrior's impulses. Though he fights without finesse, he will nonetheless strive to save the booty while torching the hut. Too, Jungle Tortoise has prepared me for this day, and I am ready to help you defend Quetzal Serpent; the city that will lead the way to a stable, happy tomorrow, free from destruction."

Before Smoke Macaw could express surprise at or disapproval of this declaration, from seemingly nowhere Jungle Tortoise appeared next to Lady Rainbow; *As if summoned by the presence of his name on my lips*, she thought. In fond greeting, he took her hands in his.

Though Smoke Macaw trusted the judgement of his truly prescient shaman-priest, and so offered no argument, still he could not help but fear the possible injury or even death in combat of the woman he loved. He therefore turned away from her, the easier to focus his attention on Quetzal Serpent itself. *Our fate must be decided soon*, he thought. *Queen Death Bat will not graciously accept a defeat, and so I may face a dilemma: if not mortally wounded or put to death in an ensuing sacrifice – which is against our ethos – she will have to be held by us in permanent imprisonment. Otherwise, subject to her continued harassment, our city state, even here on the high plateau, may finally succumb to exhaustion through attrition, just as jagged cliff boulders, once fallen and trapped in a river's course, are eventually worn smooth and round by the unceasing flow of water against them.*

The day of the contest arrived. Four figures took their places atop the combat platform: Smoke Macaw and Lady Rainbow on one side of a chalk line, and on the other side Bone Drum (as Lady Rainbow had predicted) and Queen Death Bat, the latter having also decided to participate directly. The men faced each other, as did the women. Around them was a demarcation ring of cut brush; low enough to jump over to reach the safety of neutral territory, but with thorns and pointed branch-ends that would lacerate any exposed area of skin should a combatant stumble onto them or be pushed into retreat there. Each warrior wore a tunic of double-layered thick cotton, padded with rock salt to absorb the slash of a longknife blade or the thrust of a spear tip; and a close-fitting, rounded helmet of wood and leather, its prominent rim band decorated with colourful cloth, to protect their head. A circular shield, its top the shape of a half-star (symbolic of Venus of War), a spear, and a longknife in the long red sash completed the equipment.

Smoke Macaw tested his and Lady Rainbow's weapons,

gently pricking and drawing them across the skin at his shoulder: the points were sharp and the edges honed. He regretted the mortal finality inherent in their character, for he did not wish injury or even death to occur as a result of this combat. *Too, the presence of such weapons today,* he thought, *may be interpreted by some as setting a precedent for bloodletting in Mayan society, regardless of the outcome of this combat.* He was struck again by Queen Death Bat's handsomeness, and wondered if he would really be able to take her life, despite her being a potentially lethal opponent. He had very nearly done so once before: on board her canoe at Eastern Rock. *A wall of solid air,* he recalled, *seemed to suddenly rise up between us, admonishing me and protecting her.*

At the platform's edges, near their respective teams, stood Jungle Tortoise and a priest from Black Stone, the latter of whom was to officiate in place of Nine Stars, bedridden and extremely weak following his encounter with the fer-de-lance in the pit. The simple, block-like platform had spontaneously acquired buttressed sides, formed from the hundreds of spectators pressing forward and leaning inwards. *Viewed from above by Kuch, the black vulture,* thought Smoke Macaw, *the platform would seem a living board game, its pieces shuffling their feet and swaying their torsos, readying themselves to deliver and deflect blows.*

Some of the spectators, aware of the personal significance of this contest for the four combatants, could guess at the thoughts and hopes reflected on their faces: Bone Drum's desire to acquire Lady Rainbow as his prize, Lady Rainbow's repulsion towards him, and Smoke Macaw's determination to not lose his bride-to-be. Looming above all of this was

Queen Death Bat's vision of Smoke Macaw as the co-ruler of her city.

The Queen was handicapped by her deteriorating left eye. She was too proud to ask for Jungle Tortoise's medical advice, though he surely would have given it, believing that no patient, regardless of their moral or political provenance, should be denied the right to healing. The eye was covered by a large black patch.

My training under Jungle Tortoise, and Queen Death Bat's loss of an eye, reflected Lady Rainbow, *may well conspire against the ruler of Black Stone, rendering her unable to defeat me in combat.* Her spirit was transported back in time to her training retreats, and her memories raced against the brief time remaining before the combatants would engage each other. Accompanied by two acolytes to serve as a porter and a cook, but otherwise far from the distractions of the court and the constant, bee-like humming of her adopted city, Lady Rainbow had studied with Jungle Tortoise. Initially, the prospect of entering into combat with the warrior Queen had left her feeling like an exposed crab on an open beach, its scuttling body suddenly petrifying as it became aware of a human approaching it. Under the shaman-priest's tutelage, however, she had learned to rise up against the menace that was before her once again.

"It is in the nature of all humans," Jungle Tortoise had told her, in the mountain cave that was their first retreat, "that our doubts and our dreams by turns unsettle and reassure us. Here, you will learn how to react in a new way to the constant flow of your thoughts; to distinguish between the detritus in your head – the dead leaves and withered sticks drifting at random on your mind's river – and the bobbing, delicately beautiful flower petals of life-affirming thoughts and of inspiration."

Thus it had transpired, and Lady Rainbow had soon learned that fear was, in fact, an enemy greater than Queen Death Bat. "To no longer be a slave to the whims of our emotions," she shared with her mentor one day, "we should not cling overly to even our most beautiful experiences in life, but rather, in looking back upon them, behold all our joys and our sadnesses from a bridge of calm. For, the more we try to resist change, the more painful is the moment when that which is precious to us slips away, as water will always escape clutching hands."

Jungle Tortoise was well pleased with this insight, and with those that followed. Lady Rainbow determined, as he advised, to unclutter her mind a little more each day; a skill that could bring much-needed peace in times of internal or external crisis.

At the second retreat, in a hut in the forest around Quetzal Serpent, Lady Rainbow had acquired more physically practical skills: she observed how different creatures attack or flee, many of them perfectly in tune with the grazing habits of their prey or the hunting habits of their predators, in the struggle for continued life. She learned defence and attack – bare-handed and with weapons – without fear or impulsiveness, and was frequently reminded by Jungle Tortoise that the primary objective was to immobilise one's opponent, not to take their life.

"There is no honour in arbitrary killing," he had told her. "Disarm rather than wound, wound rather than maim, maim rather than kill. Anger and thoughts of revenge are fleeting weapons in one-to-one combat. If your opponent survives their spent force, what weapons will you have left? In such cases, only the subtler forces of cunning and tenacity may help you to prevail. The successful warrior fights methodically, looking for any weakness in their opponent. They imagine that they are one with their opponent's approaching weapon, dodging it at the last moment and using the opponent's momentum against them, then responding with a counter-blow. A warrior should, like the animals, conserve their energy wherever possible, using it to attack only at the opportune moment of an opening, or when their opponent shows signs of tiring. Then can their patience be finally transformed into a storm of blows that penetrates the opponent's defensive space."

Too, in the time Lady Rainbow had spent alone with him, a previous wish of hers had been fulfilled: she had grown to know Jungle Tortoise well. He had become for her almost a second father, as he had been to Smoke Macaw and Twin Iguanas, his relationship with whom had matured into one of mutual reverence, yet with undiminished affection.

Now, on the battle platform, Bone Drum tried unsuccessfully to attract Lady Rainbow's attention. *I still desire her, and will, after Queen Death Bat has punished her, claim her as my booty following her team's defeat*, he thought. *The warrior Queen has assured me of the outcome of this contest: that Smoke Macaw will surrender upon grasping the danger to which he has allowed Lady Rainbow to expose herself. I will then take her to Place of the Tick, one of the settlements on the plain which, with Black Stone's patronage, I will raise to greatness as part of Queen Death Bat's empire, and Lady Rainbow will become my Queen.*

He turned to look at Smoke Macaw, who, glaring at him

as if he had read his thoughts, said, "We will soon be as two competing grey hawks, you and I, wheeling about a compact forest crown of spear shafts, and one must lose his place in the air and plummet to the ground." Smoke Macaw then recalled one of Jungle Tortoise's principal techniques for one-to-one combat: drawing with the eyes the basic outline of a pyramid, its three sides behind the head of one's opponent. This allowed the armed 'artist' to exploit that time-space between his opponent's mental commitment to his next action and its actual execution. Thus could the observant warrior either act pre-emptively or prepare an appropriate response to the foreseeable attack.

The two priests moved away from their teams and faced the spectators to explain the rules of the contest. So far, Black Stone's temporary priest had not convinced in his unpractised role as religious spokesperson for his city state. He knew that Queen Death Bat intended to name Jungle Tortoise as her astronomer-priest once Quetzal Serpent's defeat had been witnessed at this public platform. The unknown priest – standing next to Jungle Tortoise, whose name was legendary among the Maya of the region – straightened his shoulders, raised his head, and tried to project more power into his less-than-commanding voice. "This is an open-rules contest," he began, "in which battle cries are allowed, as is full-body contact. A fallen opponent may be struck while still on the ground. The winner will be the team whose fighter or fighters last remain standing, thus winning for their territory the title of Supreme City State of the Mayan Lands. Queen Death Bat, in her great magnanimity, has decreed that the losing team may keep their heads; in return, however, their lips will swear unquestioning obedience to their new Queen."

Smoke Macaw looked at Lady Rainbow. They both smiled grimly, for they understood Queen Death Bat's apparently merciful stance: for her to kill Smoke Macaw would be to sever one of her own limbs, and Bone Drum could have no use for a dead Lady Rainbow. Thus, as Lady Rainbow had predicted, it was certain that the combatants from Black Stone would try to inflict minimal injury upon their coveted opponents.

Now spoke Jungle Tortoise. "People of the forest, of the Great Plain, of the coast, and of our own high plateau, King Smoke Macaw's eyes are not hungry for a feast of wounded bodies, today or any other day. He wishes words could be the more persuasive weapon, a truce with Black Stone deciding the future of all our territories. 'Peace', however, is not a word Queen Death Bat will ever utter, for domination is her creed. With no other way of ceasing animosity, we have agreed to meet the aggressor here and fight before you. However, Maya, be warned: should Quetzal Serpent become Queen Death Bat's, only the fewest of her new subjects will lead a happy life. Do not think that the warrior Queen will permit any autonomy to her former allies, for nothing less than total, centralised power is surely her goal."

Here, Bone Drum looked questioningly at Queen Death Bat, but her angry eyes turned away from him.

"Therefore, reflect on this: should Queen Death Bat's team prevail, would not a future alliance of resistance to Black Stone and its ruler, even risking perhaps one's own death in the struggle, be preferable to a life as a mere worm to be continually pecked at, or even swallowed? Guests of today, do not allow yourselves to become the slaves of tomorrow."

Inwardly, Queen Death Bat cursed Jungle Tortoise as she

heard his words repeated among the spectators. *No matter*, she consoled herself. *When the contest is over, Jungle Tortoise will become loyal to Black Stone, following Smoke Macaw's instructions given in my name.*

Both seashells were blown simultaneously, three times, to signal the start of the contest. The teams moved cautiously towards each other. Each combatant studied their counterpart's sense of balance, trying to get a feel for their individual style of movement. Queen Death Bat noticed Lady Rainbow's restless eyes and, following their line of sight, guessed her plan: to penetrate an opening, place herself behind Queen Death Bat and Bone Drum, and then attack. Smoke Macaw would attack simultaneously from the front. Queen Death Bat acted first, however. She ran forward and leapt at Lady Rainbow with her spear. The spear would probably have embedded itself in Lady Rainbow's tunic, had not the wearer shifted at the last moment, transforming the relatively broad target of her body into a thin strip of clothing and flesh which the spear merely grazed; a glancing blow. The warrior Queen was left-handed, and the shield in her right hand, its front etched with the profile of an open-mouthed skull, met that etched with the head of a rattlesnake in Lady Rainbow's left. Thus the skull and the rattlesnake exchanged a brutal kiss as the shields collided. Lady Rainbow, though knocked backwards by the impact, radiated self-confidence. *My training in timing has just proven its worth*, she thought, with gratitude towards Jungle Tortoise.

Her opponent tottered from the force of her own deflected energy. "Treacherous tunic," murmured Queen Death Bat. "Its salt-filled weight has robbed me of some of my agility."

Bone Drum, hoping to maintain pressure on the other team, lunged with his spear at Smoke Macaw's head. Smoke Macaw deflected the spear with his shield while raising his stone mace. Though Bone Drum's spear remained for only the shortest of instants on the star-cleft of his shield, it was long enough for Smoke Macaw to bring down his mace upon the lodged weapon, separating the spear's head from its shaft. Bone Drum dropped the decapitated spear, retreated, and drew out his longknife. Queen Death Bat was quickly at his side, her own spear resting on the ground beside her and her stone axe in her hand. In a prearranged movement, they held together their shields and slowly advanced on their opponents. Forgetting Jungle Tortoise's philosophy of the cautious warrior, Lady Rainbow charged them, hoping to break through the moving wall with her shield and so give Smoke Macaw a more open area for attack. Suddenly, the two enemy shields were raised, throwing her to the ground.

I was a fool, she thought. *I have allowed them to use my own strategy against me.*

Queen Death Bat raised her axe and moved towards the prostrate Lady Rainbow. Bone Drum blocked the path of Smoke Macaw, who was moving to aid his betrothed. Lady Rainbow experienced her fall as a rebuke and, with her overconfidence shaken from her, realised that she had to discipline herself. As she rolled out of the striking space, the warrior Queen's axe arced through empty air and hit the stone platform, the ensuing painful vibrations causing her to drop her weapon and nurse her shocked hand with her other.

Smoke Macaw stabbed methodically at Bone Drum, who was retreating. "Lady Rainbow," he called out, "stay close behind me and shield yourself and me from Queen Death Bat."

I must remove my tunic, thought Queen Death Bat, *for greater ease of movement is essential now.* Unburdened, she began swinging her axe at Lady Rainbow, the air alive with the sound of slicing movements. Her upper body's regained freedom allowed Queen Death Bat to put more weight behind her blows and to strike Lady Rainbow's shield more often. When she felt her already jarred dominant arm begin to tire, she half turned, her rear leg now her leading leg. Supporting her aching hand against her chest, she would now have to use her naturally weaker, though undamaged, right hand to continue delivering blows. Her subsequent attacks were technically correct but without the necessary crushing force, and Lady Rainbow deflected them easily, though she peered past her shield after each: should Queen Death Bat's injured hand recover, it might attempt to grab one of the star-points of the as yet unyielding shield.

The four figures moved in a wavering line of attacks, dodges and counter-blows, Bone Drum's longknife and shield unable to stop Smoke Macaw's advance, and a one-handed Queen Death Bat unable to dislodge his rearguard of Lady Rainbow. One of Bone Drum's legs became caught in a section of the brush demarcating the arena's edge. He soon disengaged it, but Smoke Macaw was able to use the moment of inattention to push him, causing Bone Drum to stumble over the brush and fall to the ground outside the ring. Smoke Macaw turned and, seeing Lady Rainbow losing ground to Queen Death Bat, pushed the former to one side. As the Queen's spear entered his space, he ducked; sensing a lack of urgency in the thrust, he deduced that she had aimed a non-lethal strike at his shoulder. As fast as he had ducked, he arose again and, drawing Queen Death Bat towards him using her own spear, yanked it out of her relatively unpractised right hand. The punch that he then delivered connected partly with her temple and partly with the rim of her helmet, the force of the measured blow nonetheless skinning his knuckles. Fearful that the resilient warrior in front of him would recover quickly, he struck again, this time to the other side of her head. An indefinable sound issued from Queen Death Bat's mouth: half gasp, half sigh. Her arms dropped to her sides, her axe leaving her hand and falling softly to the ground. *She has become punch-drunk*, thought Smoke Macaw.

He heard Lady Rainbow yell his name and instinctively he dropped down, simultaneously rolling away. He reorientated his head and raised his mace in defence. Neither seeing nor feeling a weapon searching for his form, he half-rose into a squat. Bone Drum was back in the arena, poised to deliver a thrust with his longknife, but his posture was not supple: it was set hard, for the moment of release had been lost to him when his target had moved out of range. Smoke Macaw stood up. Keeping Queen Death Bat at the edge of her field of vision, Lady Rainbow approached the two male warriors, so as to be close enough to aid Smoke Macaw if necessary. The enthusiastic noises from the spectators had become a war chant, which gave the men fresh inspiration. Their fighting skills were equal, though different: Bone Drum had great strength, while Smoke Macaw was extraordinarily nimble. They exchanged blows many times, each warrior first striking, then bringing up his shield to receive his adversary's counter-blow.

After a time, Bone Drum noticed a change in their combat. *Smoke Macaw is becoming ever harder to engage; he and his shield simply aren't where they should be to receive my blows.* He began to feel that he was alone, merely shadow-fighting, for his glances beyond his shield revealed only empty space. He recalled that Queen Death Bat had warned him of this tactic, developed by Jungle Tortoise. Suddenly, he felt a coolness against the nape of his neck: Smoke Macaw's stone mace. Bone Drum had felt no braking movement, no impact, and yet the weapon's round head was resting snugly in the pit just below his skull. He dropped his own weapon immediately. Both men looked at Queen Death Bat, curious to see if she had registered the sudden cessation of the din of combat; if she had witnessed her teammate's defeat.

Her eyes were still fixed on the ground, but she was no longer stunned. She raised her head and blinked hard. "You twice hit my regal head with your bare hands, Smoke Macaw. The man who was to press upon my face only kisses; the ruler with whom I wanted to share my throne. Too, I have today for the first time seen for myself your dedication to Lady Rainbow, and hers to you. I see that my adversaries are not two, but one united being, and thus all the stronger." She looked in admiration and envy at the couple who were promised to each other.

Are these flattering words, wondered Smoke Macaw, *merely potter's hands working the clay of trickery, shaping a new attack upon myself and my beloved, now that urgency's pulse of survival has slowed within us?* However, he realised, after he had struck her Queen Death Bat had cried out in a pain that was not physical; her very soul had suffered from his double punch. From the emptiness in her eyes, he deduced that her inaction was a symptom of resignation, not a veiled strategy.

Queen Death Bat walked up to Bone Drum. "Give me your hipknife, Bone Drum," she commanded.

Handing it over, he looked at her with infinite suspicion: he had not forgotten what her displeasure had unleashed upon Nine Stars. With both hands, she raised the hipknife high, tip down, between herself and Bone Drum, he unable to believe that she would put him to death unannounced – they were, or had been, allies; they had this very day fought side by side for her city state. Bracing himself to receive the Queen's spontaneous sentence, he looked up and saw the blade quiver before beginning its descent.

Then a scream of agony and fury deafened him, and he stepped back. *Surely, I am hearing the echo of my own death-screams as I plummet from the Middle Realm towards Xibalba*, he thought. *But why, then, is the face before me contorted; why are the eyes of my executioneress fearful?* Save for a breastcloth, Queen Death Bat's torso was bare and unprotected. Bone Drum saw blood around the area of her belly, though the wound itself was not visible behind her hands, which still held the hipknife in place there.

With difficulty, she spoke. "Even if Black Stone were to win this contest today, I know now that the true prize – your affection, Smoke Macaw – would always be denied me. Thus, I have beheaded reclining, beckoning love – my self-delusion – and am ready to sacrifice myself to the engulfing jaws of eternal loneliness."

Queen Death Bat had tried to destroy her, it was true, but as she reflected on the other woman's butchery of her own body, Lady Rainbow felt vomit rising to the top of her throat, the acidic taste a fitting expression of her tainted compassion for her erstwhile oppressor and present opponent. She managed to repress the vomit's discharge from her mouth, but the tear that broke from one eye she allowed to continue its course down her cheek.

The warrior Queen began to collapse, and Bone Drum hurried to support her. Queen Death Bat looked up at the sky. "Both my namesake, Zotz the Death Bat, and my planned future object of worship, the star goddess Lahun Chan have forsaken me today, when I counted on their aegis the most. In my turn, I renounce them. Too, I have just betrayed my own life force, and so, as a deceased ruler, will be unable to overcome the lords of Xibalba and earn my place in the sky, reborn as one of the stars. Oh, Ixtab, goddess of suicide, accept therefore my self-sacrifice and take me unto you. Deify me as your herald, so that, though I have not acquired an earthly empire, I may, in recompense, be granted a place among… the pantheon of the Mayan gods."

Her head fell forward, and in its intensity, her last exhalation, the draught of death, sent a chill through Smoke Macaw and Bone Drum as they held her. Silent now were the throats and tongues of the spectators, struck dumb by this unexpected climax. The three surviving warriors were now at close range to each other. His thoughts elsewhere, Smoke Macaw played awhile with the mace in his hands, as if it were merely a toy. Then he tossed it to the ground. When he linked his hands behind his back, Lady Rainbow and Jungle Tortoise stepped forward, ready to intervene if necessary in their King's spontaneous game of chance.

Smoke Macaw addressed Bone Drum. "I am unarmed. If

you wish you may try again to pierce me with your spear, and this time you may succeed."

But Bone Drum showed no interest in further combat – as Smoke Macaw had predicted.

So the King said, in fitting quietness, "Let us, Queen Death Bat's ally and adversary, now join forces and act to ensure her comfort in death."

They laid her upon her back and crossed her arms over her breasts. Both her temporary lover and her true desire looked down for a while at the lifeless eyes of the once so vital warrior Queen, whose utterances in life had seemed almost darkly magical. Lady Rainbow, in her turn, watched the men. She wondered if Smoke Macaw noticed, as she did, that Bone Drum's face showed a slight softness; an expression that she recognised as sadness. Then she removed her own padded vest and placed it gently under the Queen's head. A respectful silence followed, observed by the high-born and low-born alike. This time of mourning by some and reflection by others created in many of them a shared sense of destiny.

Bone Drum ended the vigil. His voice seemed almost deafening in contrast to the hitherto total lack of sound. "I, the outcast of New Dawn, am a man without a home," he confirmed. "I have only a small company of warriors as compatriots."

"Indeed," agreed Smoke Macaw. "The buds of your new life blossomed with promise in the seemingly nurturing soil of Black Stone, only to be starved of the sun by the shadow of defeat looming over you, foretelling the fall of Queen Death Bat."

Two minor rulers from the plain climbed the platform steps and spoke to the crowd. "Queen Death Bat has failed us," said one. "She promised the lesser city states a glorious future under her leadership. We cannot return to our Chac-mouthed stone gates empty-handed." Here he looked at Bone Drum.

"Yes," agreed the other. "The decapitation on our temple steps of Queen Death Bat's favoured warrior will be necessary to calm our peoples' disappointment and anger, and to appease our gods of battle."

Smoke Macaw motioned to them to join him. "These rulers," he said, "claim that a human head and a few bowls of blood will compensate for their loss. A disproportionate and unworthy exchange: discarding as offal the remains of a great warrior! This would be an injustice to Bone Drum; though he was my enemy, he showed honour in remaining loyal to the end to Black Stone and its allies." He looked at the two rulers, to remind them of the virtue of acknowledging the greatness in one's enemy. "Blood thirsts for more blood, as sandy soil sucks away any rain that falls upon it. Smoke Macaw and Quetzal Serpent will not allow this. As victor today, I decree that Bone Drum is free to leave and re-join his men. But for where? Untrusted by and unwelcome near any Maya, they will be condemned to wander from an abandoned building here to a game-poor patch of forest there. Or the open sky may be their only roof, their food bitter berries and raw roots – a pitiful diet. A seep offering barely quenching water heated by the sun will they drink, or they will force down their throats brackish water from a coastal lagoon. As for the allies of Black Stone, they are now deprived of a benefactor. Black Stone itself lacks a ruler; the city of sparkling stone will fade as it dislodges its own door-lintels and cornerstones, its priests and warriors vying for influence and slaying one another in their attempt to become Queen Death Bat's successor."

Smoke Macaw was gratified to hear voices of agreement from below him.

"Yet there is another way," he continued, "wherein the citizens of our city states can be sure of living beyond the next few phases of the moon. People of Black Stone, you are already acquainted with Bone Drum. He has served faithfully your departed Queen, and fought at your side. Accept him as your ruler; invite his men to truly live among you and bring their knowledge and skills to bear in the new Black Stone."

Bone Drum picked up his spear and looked at Smoke Macaw as he considered his own answer. Then he held forward his spear to show his allegiance to the King of Quetzal Serpent. The two previous advocates of a sacrifice, impressed by Smoke Macaw's clemency and by Bone Drum's visible lack of bitterness towards his vanquisher, held forward their spears also. Delegates of Black Stone then ascended the platform to likewise demonstrate their agreement to Smoke Macaw's proposal.

Smoke Macaw resumed his speech of reconciliation and optimism. "Everyone here today, all waiting to experience real, lasting prosperity, acknowledge the authority of Quetzal Serpent that brings with it Smoke Macaw's benevolence and protection. Welcome, too, as General Consul to the settlements and smaller cities, my brother Twin Iguanas. He will be accompanied on his administrative journeys by his future wife, Lady Consul Yellow Knot, sister of Lady Rainbow."

Hearing this, Twin Iguanas' mouth opened in astonishment, then closed again in a broad smile. This was, for Smoke Macaw, the best thanks he could receive. The spectators cheered, sharing in Twin Iguanas' happiness. In confirmation of their betrothal, Twin Iguanas put his right hand on his heart, somewhat distractedly, as he searched for Lady Yellow Knot's face among the many below him. Lady Rainbow also smiled. While residing again at New Dawn, she – already known at court as a flawless matchmaker – had spoken to her sister of Twin Iguanas' good character and his accomplishments, both complemented by his good looks. Immediately Lady Yellow Knot had implored their father to allow her to travel with Lady Rainbow to meet the brother of Smoke Macaw. Upon their introduction Lady Rainbow's sensitivity for human compatibility had once again proved itself: Yellow Knot and Twin Iguanas could not bear to be apart for even the shortest of periods.

"Remember," said Smoke Macaw, "we will also have as an ally King Parrotfish and his city of New Dawn, ready to trade with us its harvests of the sea, as well as wares acquired from the seagoing Putún Maya." He paused, watching for doubt or dissent. He saw none. "Maya, we have two choices. We can follow our present trail, with its myriad, disorientating side trails, full of the weeds and tripping roots of empty promises that, leading nowhere, will force us to backtrack in desperation as we feud among ourselves and eventually destroy each other; or we can walk together in strength on the simpler, clearly marked trail of cooperation, our bounties to come visible ahead of us. But know this: if you choose to walk alongside Quetzal Serpent, I, its King, will abolish human sacrifice, which is as wasteful as throwing pearls – though beautiful, inedible – to the hungry, fruit-seeking toucan. Let us instead, to the gods' honour, raise buildings of beauty and solidity."

Lady Rainbow and Jungle Tortoise stepped forward, to proudly stand side by side with Smoke Macaw. His words were met with spontaneous drumming, ululations, and the stomping of spear shafts, reflecting the cultural diversity of the Mayan groups and clans present. Twin Iguanas and Bone Drum drew up behind their King, his betrothed, and Jungle Tortoise, high priest to all of them. Jungle Tortoise looked at his King out of the corner of his eye. Smoke Macaw's plan for a peacefully united Mayan region was bold and unprecedented. Could it work, he wondered?

Below the platform, there was a final exchange of options and opinions. The ensuing harmonious atmosphere Smoke Macaw allowed himself to interpret as a positive reaction to his words. "Am I right in believing that a common tomorrow has now been agreed to by all present?" he asked.

The remainder of the leaders or their delegates ascended the platform and held forward their spears.

"If you are loyal to Quetzal Serpent and to its new federation," said Smoke Macaw, "do as I do. Kneel now before the shaman-priest-astronomer Jungle Tortoise. Feel his wisdom. Know that Smoke Macaw and his allies could have no better oracle."

When Smoke Macaw arose again, he saw a field of allegiance: standing spears held by kneeling bearers. "Rise," he commanded. With his stone mace – his symbol of regal power – raised high in one hand, he walked once around the platform. "Scribes, you have also witnessed the will of the Maya present today. Write now these words: 'Smoke Macaw's holy count: day one of the many peoples being one.' "

As was customary at state events, the scribes were already seated in a cleared space before the platform. They were watched by everyone as they transcribed the royal statement into visible characters.

"Once back in the comfort of their writing rooms," concluded Smoke Macaw, "the scribes will record in detail the ceremonial battle just fought, and the resulting start of a new era in our history."

The leaders and delegates left the platform, and the intermingled spectators re-formed into their original groups. The excitement of the day and the promising outcome of the contest bestowed power upon each person's steps as they began their journey back to their city or settlement. Soon only Quetzal Serpent's retinue remained, conversing with cheerful pride as they waited a short distance away for their King. Smoke Macaw felt the tension, the heavy cloak of office, slip from his shoulders as he approached the people closest to him: Twin Iguanas, Lady Rainbow and Jungle Tortoise.

Jungle Tortoise looked at the corpse of Queen Death Bat – lain upon a simple, open litter, Bone Drum's men setting it upon their shoulders to carry it back to Black Stone – and said reflectively, more to himself than to anyone else, "Its heady fragrance irresistible, ambition the fruit may foul and rot before it can be plucked." Looking up again, he addressed the small group before him. "At the end of the contest we saw Smoke Macaw's unarmed courage that was actually a display of self-assuredness. You, my King, sensed that Bone Drum, like his warrior Queen, had undergone a transformation, and thus would not inflict that final, eternal cut upon your body. He understood that his alliance with Queen Death Bat could never have lasted, for she loved not him, but another: you."

Lady Rainbow gave Smoke Macaw a kindly, understanding glance that showed no jealousy.

"Moreover," continued Jungle Tortoise, "I think he suspected some future trickery from her in her dealings with him; that he might one day be in danger. Her self-induced death deepened his feeling of non-belonging, so that he decided to try, perhaps for the last time, to create a new life for himself and his company of warriors. The wisdom of Smoke Macaw has allowed him to do this."

"I thank you, Jungle Tortoise," replied Smoke Macaw. "To recognise the virtues of one's subjects is one of the duties of a ruler; to be able to exercise these virtues to the fullest is, in its turn, the greatest privilege that can be bestowed upon any person who wishes to live more than a mere shadow of a life."

Here Lady Rainbow thought of Rain God on the Wind, whom she had come to consider a friend. He had transcended his humble beginnings, reaching at Quetzal Serpent an elevated, unique status. *In sacrificing his own life to protect mine*, she reflected, *he reciprocated to the highest degree that gift – the opportunity of self-realisation – once bestowed upon him by his King.*

"Under the gracious aegis of Smoke Macaw," Rain God on the Wind had once said to Lady Rainbow, "I was transformed from a common ear of maize in a field, to a living manifestation of the rain god Chac."

Chapter 27

From the Tattoos of Doom Emerges Beauty

From Quetzal Serpent's temple summit there looked out over the landscape an animal figure in red. The points on its body by turns glinted and faded, depending on the whim of the clouds that chose either to leave exposed or to obscure the sun.

The *Kul Balam*, the Sacred Jaguar. The theft of its Heart had set in motion a sequence of unprecedented events. Never before had a human swum to the bottom of a cenote, and sexual desecration of royalty had hitherto been unknown. No record existed of a ruler taking their own life; such disrespect for the breath of the gods in one's own body would anger the Earth Monster, causing it to shake the transgressing city to its foundations, razing it to the ground. Every citizen of Quetzal Serpent appreciated the rightness, the inevitability of this cycle that now culminated in the celebratory presentation of the Sacred Jaguar.

Below the idol stood Smoke Macaw and Lady Rainbow. Seemingly growing out of the King's head were three tall green plumes from a resplendent quetzal – plucked harmlessly, recalled Smoke Macaw with satisfaction, for they would grow back in time for the bird's next mating season. Lady Rainbow wore a multicoloured gown depicting coral and fish. Strung about her neck was a pendant of large bars of red coral; a wedding gift from her father. Copal incense smoke rose from a brazier behind them, and on the projecting dais stood Jungle Tortoise.

"My subjects," said King Smoke Macaw, "Green-Eyed Lady Rainbow is the other half that makes me whole as a man and as a ruler. Her earthly trials, especially at the will of Queen Death Bat, have been equal to the torments endured by the Heroic Twins and by deceased rulers at the hands of the demons of Xibalba."

Lady Rainbow stepped in front of him for a moment, he willingly eclipsed by her, and a cheer arose from the assembled populace. Drawing up alongside her again, Smoke Macaw held out his open palm. She placed hers upon his, and they joined Jungle Tortoise at the dais.

"These two royal betrothed," said the shaman-priest, "are now blessed by me in the unbroken sharing of their lives. I declare my unfailing dedication to them. May all subjects of Quetzal Serpent echo my spoken seal of the union of Smoke Macaw and Green-Eyed Lady Rainbow."

A second cheer – even more forceful than the first; its wake reverberating through the acoustically hollow temple stones – fulfilled Jungle Tortoise's request.

The King and his Queen descended to the base of the temple, where they were showered with orchid petals. Lady Rainbow let her robe fall to her feet. Clad now in only a breastcloth and a loincloth of Maya blue, she turned to face Smoke Macaw. With deliberate slowness, they brought their heads nearer and nearer, and finally kissed. As was expected of newlyweds, they then held their hands to their ears in mock sensitivity to the volume of the ensuing third cheer. Lady Rainbow looked proudly at her arms and legs, and smiled at Smoke Macaw. As promised, he had had the bat tattoos, engraved onto her limbs at the Cave of the Bats, transformed into something beautiful. The razor-toothed mouth and the jagged black wings of Zotz the Death Bat had disappeared. In their place could now be seen the delicate head and wings of that omen of happiness, the blue morpho butterfly.

This book is printed on paper from sustainable sources managed under the Forest Stewardship Council (FSC) scheme.

It has been printed in the UK to reduce transportation miles and their impact upon the environment.

For every new title that Matador publishes, we plant a tree to offset CO_2, partnering with the More Trees scheme.

For more about how Matador offsets its environmental impact, see www.troubador.co.uk/about/